The Peacock Room

CATIE JARVIS

ISBN: 1-988292-04-5
ISBN-13: 978-1-988292-04-5

For my mom, my dad, and my sister, who always believed in all my stories…

ACKNOWLEDGMENTS

My thanks to the writing faculty at Ithaca College, who worked on an extremely rough and longwinded 500-page version of this novel with me so many years ago.

Gratitude to the brilliant professors at California College of the Arts, especially John Laskey, Tom Barbash, Cooley Windsor, Aimee Phan, and Anne Marino, who took careful time with me, and through this novel taught me how to edit a novel, which is perhaps the most difficult art of all.

Thank you to Michael Vicchitto, who edited countless versions of this novel, and whom I wrote this book alongside and for.

Thank you to my family and dearest friends, near and far, here and ether, who have, for as long as I have known them, encouraged my writing with sincerity, support, and love: Kyla, Patty, Shannon, Sarah, Phil, Aunt Debbie, Uncle Hank, Grammy and Poppy.

Much appreciation for Hyperborea Publishing, and thanks to Raphael Deketele for your time and care in producing this novel.

Movement I

Move the shoulders,
Shake the arms!
And the noon wind
Breathes in the face!

Aleksey Koltsov
("Song of the Reaper")

CHAPTER ONE

Jonis Stark stopped to observe the lonely shoe. It was the beginning of a humid August in "the year of strong interaction," as Jonis called it, referring to the year's notable discovery in physics of the force that ties together the smallest of nature's particles. Jonis stood in the middle of the Ithaca commons in upstate New York, where downtown storefronts and offices were still dark and vacant. The morning sun announced itself in a red vibrato: *Look at me! I rise and rise!!* He watched the light seep over the single black platform sandal, certain that things in pairs, once separated, could never leave their loneliness.

Jonis had contemplated this idea extensively, imagining empty space where his mass of leg resided. His right leg was tender and irregular, a string of raw red meat slapped together in a meandering chain by a careless butcher. It was heavy and hard to forget. He had all of the memories of it being with him and none of its absence. If he could envision the leg gone, it might be possible to part with it. At times throughout his life he longed for lightness and mobility. But he had come so far with this leg as part of himself.

Jonis's memories of possessing a "normal" leg were

few: fuzzy images of a small neat foot, missing three of the five metatarsals but still hardly disfigured. Some months after Jonis and I had met, he showed me snapshots of his childhood self. "Look, Lizzy," he said to me. "Look at what I was." The pictures were of a variety now almost obsolete: Kodak film developed at the local drug store and Polaroids shaken into magical existence. "The last batch of children not saved on hard drives," I said. "I like to think that makes us precious."

The pictures showed Jonis in action, running, jumping, rolling round-faced down a hill. They showed his short shapely calves, both matching in size, and that telling port-wine birthmark running down the right leg like a map of South America, thick at the top and thinning into a long triangle. "'Where to?' my mother would ask playfully when I was young," he told me as he flipped from one photograph to the next. "She'd trace her finger over the mark, warning, 'Some day soon your leg may change very fast,' as if she and the doctors could predict its future. She lied and promised that it would be beautiful." I would have liked to interject that it was beautiful, but he didn't wait long enough between phrases. "I feel there is a version of me that will always be that young boy," he said, "standing perfectly on that hill." He held the photos before me as proof that he had not always been different, but had become it. Jonis was always trying to be usual, whereas I longed for just the opposite. I saw these pictures as hopeful evidence that a regular boy in blue and white high-tops could become something so unexpected.

Jonis dropped his crutches in the street on that August morning, his first morning living in this new small city just a few hours southwest of the high-rises and bustle of Syracuse, where he'd been residing for the previous six years. His crutches were custom-made, with soft arm cushions and springy pads at the feet, but this once he discarded them carelessly. He reached for the shoe. It was damp within his hands from morning dew. It dangled from its strapped arch, swinging between index, middle, and thumb. The shoe was scuffed at the toe from a trip on the sidewalk or a long night of dancing. It was a right shoe, the kind Jonis had hardly known. His shoes never had their pair: lone right counterparts sat untouched in the closets of his life. He had seen such shoes before on slender sloping feet, small, neat feet, painted red toes, tender brown, cream, or black skin, never red skin patched in varicose veins, birthmark stains, and pinheads of blood. No girl that he loved had skin like his. And would it have revolted him if she did? Could he love a girl who could never hope to fit in this shoe? Could he love a girl who would fit too easily?

The doctors who monitored Jonis monthly from birth knew to expect disfigurement, an enlarged foot, and fleshy tumors. They foresaw that the leg would end up too long for Jonis's eventual height of five foot eleven. But they were still awed by the outcome, by the way his leg extended, all thirty-three inches of elongated tibia, and four pounds of fleshy tumor growth that spread out wide and down to his foot.

Jonis was diagnosed with one syndrome and then another, each fitting somehow though never quite right. "You're an anomaly," Dr. Kershner said proudly, though his sense of satisfaction would eventually fade. Each diagnosis held commonalities: diseases of disfigurement, rarity, complexity. Diseases that resulted from a mutated gene, one slight mishap in a sea of stern, organized cells. Diseases without instructions on cure save the risky removal of a limb altogether.

The growth began with his long elegant tibia and encompassed the muscles, tissues, and veins from the knee cascading toward the foot. The area increased in length slowly during some periods of his life and more quickly at others. His leg grew as he did, into his long nose, large eyes, and lanky limbs. A battle of constant growing pains; it hurt, he said, like an internal brawl – his leg versus the rest of him, bone versus flesh, or perhaps his mother versus the doctors – punch, probe, jab. He never knew who to root for.

Jonis was consumed by the image of a beautifully footed girl bewildered in a dark room, a girl not accustomed to having only one shoe on her feet. "Where could I have lost it?" she was asking, like Cinderella. He knew the answer but he was not her savior. The shoe belonged to him now, to possess and to ponder. For in this world certain things need observing; their flaws, dilapidation, and beauty can expose us to our own.

On that same August morning, a few hours later and a few blocks south from where Jonis had been roaming, still a stranger unknown to me, I stared into a mirror and watched sadness lodge itself in my jaw and eyes. I pretended that I was an actress in a soap opera named Regina whose lover had left me for my best friend on the same day my father was killed in a car accident. As the tears poured from my eyes, I felt more sorrow for *Regina* than I ever could have felt for myself. In that moment my own life reverberated with a void that I couldn't place, and I was irritated, even infuriated by the unknowing.

The phone rang four times before my roommate picked it up.

"Liiiiiiiiiizzyyyyyy!" Inka called from the living room, lingering on an *A* and dropping down.

"Coming out," I called back. I blew my nose and shook out my matted hair.

"It's some woman named Patty…" Inka whispered, pushing the phone at me.

She took quick note of my blotchy eyes but decided to ignore them.

"Shit," I whispered back, "I can't talk to her yet."

"Hi, Patty," Inka began into the phone, "Lizzy just hopped in the shower. I'll let her know that you called."

Inka pulled the phone away as the woman on the other end continued speaking at an excessive volume until Inka hung up on her. The woman had left three messages in the past two days and I hadn't returned any of them.

"She says to call her back as soon as possible: it's 'very important' that she hears from you." Inka leaned forward, wagged her finger with mocking authority. The gesture was unnerving, her head and chest threatened to topple over her lanky limbs, and I was relieved when she stood back upright.

"It's about that piano," I explained.

"Get it! We'll put it in the kitchen, in place of the fridge and stove. We'll lose weight."

"That's not helpful."

The piano had been left to me by Mrs. Malburn, who was stern, slender, and old with creases in her face as thick and right as pre-Columbian etchings that had triumphed over time. She was the only dance teacher I knew who still hired musicians to play for her classes so the children could dance to live music – an outdated tradition. Having a piano stop and start to your very movement was a sensation that an iPod could never replicate. Now, following Mrs. Malburn's death, the old dance studio had been bought up by a businesswoman, Patty Stark – apparently a woman with no use and no patience for the large musical instrument. Her messages informed me that I either had to come take it or she'd get rid of it herself.

Inka mixed us some rum and Coke, an afternoon snack good for a hot Saturday, and we headed out to the porch. We sunk into recliners we'd swiped cheap from a weekend garage sale, and gazed at the rows of overgrown oak trees. Our yard was small but grassy and Columbia Street, which it overlooked, was not heavily trafficked. The apartment above ours had been vacant since May, when the student living there left town after graduation. For the time being the whole porch and yard belonged to us to do with as we pleased. We never had to worry about playing our music too loud or about inviting over friends for late-night parties, although the social scene had thinned with the onset of summer.

After graduation there had been a mass exodus. The recent graduates landed jobs that scattered them across American metropolitan centers. They returned to preserved childhood bedrooms as tenants on an open-ended lease, went to study abroad, or were accepted into this or that graduate school. Few had decided to linger. But I, unlike most of the students, was practically a local, raised in a small town called Endicott not a half-hour away. I had built up a solid catalog of piano tuning clients, and it made sense for me to stick around and continue to cultivate my business. Inka had secured a decent job at the college as an assistant in the bursar's office, early mornings and one annoying boss, but she only had to work part days on Fridays and got the weekends off. So, as the others dispersed, it was mostly Inka and me, hanging on the porch, walking through the parks, having dinner and drinks downtown. The world seemed slower, more intimate than it had been a few months before when we were still in school. We often sat together quietly and just observed.

Across the street a guy kicked in the door of the abandoned house that had been boarded-up and overgrown for as long as anyone could remember. He kicked calmly, a steady bump-bump-bump.

"You think he'll break it down?" I asked.

"He'll get tired soon," Inka replied as if she knew.

His hair was thick and dreaded, such dedication to its form. His arms lapped the air, back and forth, and the kicking continued. We lived in a college town, and even when the semester was over, these kinds of things happened on warm weekend afternoons.

"You should take off those sunglasses – you'll be a raccoon," Inka advised.

I pulled the shades from my face, yawned twice, and wiped my watery eyes. Around three o'clock the previous night I had received a call like usual, only this time I hadn't been able to fall back to sleep. My boyfriend Joe called late at night and sang cheesy love songs with slightly inaccurate lyrics and his precise voice.

"Baby, you're all that I want. And you're lying there in my arms. I'm finding it tough to believe, we're in heaven…"

"Hi, Joe."

"Ooooooooh, love is all that I need, and I found it there in your arms. I'm trying hard to believe we're in heeeeeeaaaaveeeeen, ooooh oooooh ooooooh…"

"I love you, too, Joe. Goodnight."

I had hung up the phone and snuggled back into the blankets hiding half a smile behind my annoyance. He was very busy, I had assured myself, and it was good of him to call.

Joe led a nocturnal life, which it took all morning, afternoon, and early evening to recover from. I placed hopeless phone calls to him throughout the day; he rarely answered. I let the phone perform its seven-ring song and listened to his recorded voice and the discordant *C*-pitched "beeeeeeeep."

I left my messages in question form. The questions could be simple: *Joe, how come you never answer your phone? Joe, where are you singing right now?* Or they could be more complex: *What does it feel like to be loved by an audience? Joe, do you think it's normal for a person to cry every day?* A daily prayer, I needed to ask these questions even if no one was listening.

Joe and I saw each other once or twice a month, when we could find the time to conquer the distance between us. I lived off of potent memories. Winter. A brutal city walk. Joe refusing to look at a map even when we were lost because it was his city now and he understood it. "It's simple," he told me. *Simple like my toes losing feeling and falling off,* I thought. "All grid-like. Just follow the numbers." This was something any tri-state area kid might say. I had lived my whole life within five hours of NYC. I knew of its form well enough but I'd never claim to own it. I'd always thought that someday I'd be inside its high-rises, night-clubs, and theaters; someday I'd have lovely, talented friends on each avenue. I'd spent years imagining my life of fame in New York. Picturing Lincoln Center and the gown I would wear. When I'd lived there for years, bought a classy apartment, started a small family, then the city would be mine.

For Joe it was different. He was from the Midwest; everything in the city was an unforeseen dream for him. "I'll take you to my favorite coffee shop. You should see the things they'll mix up for you. I think it's just a few blocks from here," Joe said that night, rubbing his hands together, his cheeks pink from the cold. He'd been there a few months and he was already so sure that he belonged. I held back a shiver and ducked behind a bus stop to shield myself from the city wind. I let Joe go on believing that we would find the coffee shop soon, that we were not lost, that this was his city.

I let Joe believe I did not long for him in the days between our visits. I prided myself on never begging, bug-ging, bothering for his whereabouts, though secretly I'd been keeping a list of Joe's performances for months. It hung by a pizza advertisement magnet on my refrigerator so I knew which stage he stood upon on any given night, a small jazz club with his band, *On the Fritz*, or an immense theater as a member of the New York Opera. Inka and I took turns tracking him from internet sites and his patchy emails, and when he came to visit she or I would take the list down and place it in the miscellaneous drawer with our unspoken shame, to be returned to its place only after he departed. It hung there now, and above it was a picture of Joe in a green magnetic frame. A picture I took in the small campus apartment I shared with Inka junior year of college.

It is one of those pictures you could climb right into: the sticky air of that small space, the way that books and drafts of scribbled staff paper made it impossible to keep clean. I could summon the feeling that ran between my small intestines and spleen when I knew that Joe was going to be coming over to share his tauntingly green eyes and that voice, thick and full of deep blue and purple hues that I could feel floating through me when he spoke in his pleasant *F* to *F sharp*. Joe could sing an aria with all the passion of first love and I loved to hear him. Even late at night and miles away, I could feel his presence as if he was standing on a stage before me. I loved him most when he was dressed up and spot lit. I felt his applause as if in some way it was mine.

The guy across the street stopped kicking at the door and I sighed into the newly reinstated silence. He moved behind a shrub and dropped onto all fours, groveling. He dug around with his hands and began to collect some stones into a pile.

"Have you ever thought of shaving your pubes?" Inka said, picking ice cubes out of her drink and throwing them at the tree opposite us. She missed more often than not. "It can enhance sensitivity."

I made a little sarcastic *hm* with pulled-in lips that buzzed against my teeth. I was disappointed at Inka's reading. If anything, I felt overly sensitive, but not in the area Inka was trying to revise.

"I'm not compelled," I said.

I wished that Inka had instead asked me about the piano being offered to me, staunch and historic, with its old reverent tones. I wished she had asked of Joe, of what excitement he might be up to as we sat there on our boring porch; or even that she had asked me about the boy across the street, whether I thought he was insane or attractive with his chaotic behavior, whether I might prefer to date a boy whose life was much less put together than mine was. Anything but pubes.

"It's not hard. I'll tell you everything you need to know," Inka pressed.

"Fine," I said. I could tell by the slanting of her brows that she was ready to go right at it.

"Trim with a small pair of scissors, a close trim," she said. "Then take your razor and shave it all going from top to bottom. Then change your razor – you want a nice sharp one for this next part. Spread some conditioner on the skin and pull it tight between your hands and this time go from bottom to top, doing only small sections at a time."

By this point, I wasn't paying much attention anymore. Inka had almost finished her rum and Coke. She was a much better drinker than I was. I admired this about her.

"Make sure to keep *reee*-applying the conditioner and you'll be set," Inka said. Her over-emphasized "reeeee" brought me back to focus. Had we switched the conversation to hair conditioning? I wondered, not certain about what I had missed.

The Ivanova family spoke only Russian at home, so Inka still had a funny way of pitching certain words, as if the inflection from one language sometimes crossed over to the other without her knowing or planning for it. She tended to rise up on prefixes, piecing her words together with their root in an odd song. Whenever she said the words "rethink" or "unfair," she ended up singing the first syllable and then grunting the second. There were plenty of other words like this. Maybe she disagreed with where the emphasis lay; she was always one for doing things her own way. I took to Inka's "accent" when I became able to predict it. It was a piece of her that I could share. Often I'd drown out her words and simply listen for the shapes of her syllables, her pivots of emphasis and varying pitches; they calmed me.

"Will you do it then?" Inka asked.

"What?" I asked.

"Um, shaving your piz'da. Haven't you been listening to me?"

"I never even see Joe," I tried.

"Don't do it for him – do it for yourself."

I sighed dramatically and clinked around the ice cubes in my glass.

"So when is Joe going to get his hot ass up here again?" Inka asked.

"I don't know. Busy, busy."

Inka giggled. "I like you with Joe. It makes sense: he doesn't take up your time."

"Yeah, isn't he just *perfect*?"

Inka stood up and stretched her arms over her head towards the sun. "In some respects. Certain girls would give anything to have a charming talented boyfriend and to still be so free."

The mystery boy, or was he a man, from across the street began to throw rocks at a window. Ta, tap-tap-tap: in three with a pick-up. I wondered if we were supposed to call the cops. He threw at a constant pace from his seemingly endless supply of small stones. Some of the rocks made it to the roof, others hit the siding, but most of them smacked the glass, cracking it. Inka and I cocked our heads around to see him through the trees, his white t-shirt hiked up further and further revealing his tan back and every so often he switched throwing arms.

I watched closely and I knew him then, his yellow-green eyes, his dark and spotted skin aged from sun. I'd seen him downtown in the commons taking pictures of the sidewalk with a complicated camera, I'd seen him swimming naked at the gorges and I could picture the tight indent of his behind which I'd caught before quickly averting my eyes. He wasn't a student as I'd first taken him, but a local, a resident, like Inka and I could now claim to be. His nakedness, his freedom, it scared me. I had seen him once, balancing on the top of a slide at the town park, maybe a year before. I had wanted to see what he'd do next. Jump off, slide down, nothing? I watched for minutes, waiting on a group of friends, but when they arrived to take me away he was still balancing up there.

"Inka, I think I'm lonely," I said, reaching out as I did on occasion.

"Oh Lizzy. I've been lonely since I was five years old and my mother told me that she would refuse to speak to me unless I stopped learning 'the damned English language.' I shook my little head 'no.' She pulled my sister out of the bathroom. My sister had been peeing and her pants were down; there was a yellow stream still trickling down her leg. She turned my sister around and pulled up her shirt to show me the welts on her back. 'Is this what you want me to have to do to you?' she said to me, in Russian, of course. 'You become a bad American girl like the rest of them and this is what you will get.' And my mother didn't talk directly to me again for five years, except when she was beating me. Now *that* is lonely."

From across the road we heard a shatter, a burst of freedom. The guy bent down and lifted a sharp trapezoid of glass from the ground. He looked around and perhaps he spotted us across the pot-holed road, watching him. He tossed the shard and hurried away from the scene of the crime.

CHAPTER TWO

Patty Stark was relentless. She began to call me three or four times a day, always with the same message: "Ms. Lizzy Shulton? You need to come retrieve your piano or I will be forced to dispose of it." So, finally, I gathered my courage and set up an appointment to see about the piano.

At five to the hour, I entered the heavy metal door nestled among a strip of stores. I scaled the stairs, pausing on each for reflection: Mrs. Malburn's tightly composed bun atop her head, the ribbon ties of a point shoe, the piano keys a line of yellowed teeth. I hated being early or being late. At two minutes to the hour, I entered the waiting room where stuffy mothers used to sit and watch their daughters twirl. The walls were now painted white, instead of the bright blue they had been, and a sign across the front of the studio's door read *Stark Raving Ads*.

At one minute to the hour, I knocked.

"Come on in," called a voice, sweet and sure. It moved quickly across the air like a well-made paper airplane and settled on an *E flat*. It was a young voice, a man's voice, not the voice from my answering machine.

I cracked open the door. Filing cabinets and room dividers covered the space where ballerinas had once stood in first position. There was the same white ceiling, as chipped and water-stained as I remembered it, and that stretch of dance mirror across the front where as a child I was afraid to stare for too long, that someone might catch me and think me vain. I looked bravely, now, into that mirror, fixed my hair behind my ears, pulled my tank top down over my hips and beside my reflection I saw the head of a man emerge from behind a cubicle. His hair was tousled and fell over his face longer on the right side than the left. I wondered if that was intentional. I assumed it was. There was a long, thin scar under his left eye, a puffy moon-sliver that cupped the socket.

"Just a minute," he called out and disappeared behind the mock-walls once again.

Standing there alone, it was like being in the pink leotard all over again: conspicuous. It never fit right, that funny-shaped piece of cloth, and likewise, I never fit correctly into the world of dance. I had the hardest time remembering the steps Mrs. Malburn taught us. I would focus on the quickly changing pitches of the music until I was occupied enough to believe that no one would notice the two awkward versions of myself trying to keep up. I had a feeling that the image outside of the mirror couldn't possibly have looked as confused as the one in it. Mrs. Malburn would shake her head as I clunked away and call "Lizzy!" and then I knew for sure that my pitch finding had once again distracted me.

The man rose from behind the partition and headed towards me, his crutches propelled him. His right leg was bent at the knee and held up behind him as he moved along rhythmically. This seemed normal at first, a fractured fibula or a torn Achilles tendon, but no, that wasn't it; his right leg was peculiar and would make anyone stop and stare. It stuck out much further than a normal leg would, and at the end of the leg, there was a black bag with long straps fastened around his thigh to hold it up. I could only conceive of his foot being inside that bag – where else would his foot be? I wondered how he managed to navigate with such a strange obstruction.

His crutches moved like well-trained soldiers. They were so lustrous that I could see reflections in them as he passed: a small canister of jelly beans sitting on a desk, an odd red and silver totem statue that reached nearly to the ceiling near the door of the studio, a box on the floor labeled in bold Sharpie: *Femme Fatale*. He was absorbing all of the things around him with his strange metal prongs, pulling details of rooms and cities, pulling distorted reflections of people and artwork, onto their silver screen. In the moments that it took him to move across that small dance room it seemed that his crutches had eaten up everything in the room, every last object and fray of light, until he was all that I could see. His angular shape, his bright pale skin. I was momentarily in a universe devoid of all else.

"Hello," he said. He waited patiently for me to make my judgments.

"Lizzy," I said. "About the piano."

"Ah, the piano… My mother told me you would be coming."

He moved to me and leaned his armpit deep into his crutch so that he could offer me his hand.

"Jonis," he said and paused. "Beautiful, right? I don't know about pianos but I think it's the kind I would want if I wanted one."

I laughed. "Well, then we have something in common."

The room felt small, sectioned off and claustrophobic. The middle area, where I now stood, was obstructed by the piano and by boxes only partly unpacked.

"Looks different in here," I said, and Jonis nodded as if he had known it before, wide and empty with that echo of young laughter.

"We're still getting settled," Jonis defended, though I hadn't meant to insult. "My mother is slow to organize, and I only moved down from Syracuse this past week."

"Welcome," I said grandly, as if the whole city of Ithaca were mine.

"I'm sorry about the dance woman," he said. "Did you know her well?"

"Mrs. Malburn. She was my teacher when I was little and then I played piano for her for years after my dance career ended, through high school and college. It was a good job," I said, and I thought afterward, *It was a musician's job*, maybe the only one I'd ever have.

I walked to the piano. It looked as I'd remembered it, bold and wide with a matted horse-hide shine. It was a dark cherrywood grand piano from the '60s, the end of the era when pianos were made to last forever. Its long, thin, horizontal strings set to vibrate freely, to outlast maker and owner. A grand piano could show overtones in a way the upright I grew up with could never dream of, and this closeness to true pitch was alluring.

Upon the piano there sat a curious black high-heeled sandal. They were a sexy pair, the small vivid angles of the sandal set against the curvaceous instrument. The piano and the shoe seemed posed for an old-time photograph, where a jazz singer in a sequined dress might appear at any moment. She'd be well past her prime, this singer, face set with lines and an airy strain to her tone, fitting right into the scene of things worn and dispossessed.

I removed the shoe and placed it on the floor in order to prop the piano's lid open. Jonis made like he would explain, a grumbling in his throat.

"I found it," he said.

"It's not good to put things on top of pianos," I joked. It was a rule akin to jaywalking, which no one took seriously. Of all my clients there was only one, Jane, who kept the top of the piano bare. Even at my childhood home I couldn't talk my mother out of putting up her array of photos, mostly pictures of me playing the piano at different ages and venues.

I sat on the bench with its curved legs and bulbous

ankles, and wondered what to do: to jabber on, to swiftly depart, to summon up my strength and drag the piano out the door with me? I slid back the key's cover and gently placed my hands in formation. I played one note: *C sharp*. My favorite note. The action was soft and the note flat.

I started a little exercise using the pentatonic scale and the room filled with my sound. An old feeling return-ed to me, one I had forgotten... One cue and the dancers would begin, focused and serene, forcing the body to be light though it is heavy. Mrs. Malburn had only to nod in my direction, that sad disappointed gesture, and I would know to stop and allow her to call out her insults and corrections: "Right leg, Mindy!" "Shoulders down! I said shoulders down!" I would prepare my fingers to begin again, excited at what I could command. I was the start to the room's movement, and with the abrupt stop of my sound everything paused, dancers and teacher alike. In this room, and this room alone, the mistakes were never mine, the focus was never on me, yet every step depended on my music.

From the scales, I meandered into this part of Tchaikovsky's "The Seasons." I played "June," the most haunting of Tchaikovsky's months, a carefully suspended melody. Everything felt as slow as the notes: my thoughts and Jonis's reactions. He turned and watched me and I could feel him examine first my face and then my hands. He rested himself on the floor so quietly that I didn't hear him move but only felt him shrink. He was my private audience, and I despised such intimacy. The only person who I'd play for individually was my mother and only because she enjoyed it so much that I felt bad depriving her. Large audiences were fine, in groups people bulked together so that I couldn't tell, and maybe they couldn't tell, what they really thought. But music transferred one on one was sharp and messy – one person so quiet and the other so loud. It was hard to recover from.

I finished the section and suspended the last note,

putting off the silence as long as I could, and when the sound had trailed off to an imperceptible vibration, Jonis called out, "I loved that." He spoke loudly like I was far away and I was relieved that he attached no compliment, no immediate request for where I learned to play this way and why and how. I waited, hoping he would rise, but he did not and so I sat beside him on the floor, beneath three large windows looking out on the clean, old-fashioned streets of the Ithaca commons with their cobblestones and fountains and a serene amount of trees planted carefully in the concrete.

"That was a movement from my first-year jury," I told Jonis. "Freshman year of college, it seems so distant. It's been years since I've played it…"

On the floor Jonis's left foot twitched back and forth and his long right leg, stretched out and ending in a duffel, lay still.

"But it's still so perfect. How can you remember?"

"Thanks, but no," I said. "It's never been perfect."

I left an opening, and rather than argue, Jonis nodded sadly like an old friend. "Tell me," he said. Sitting there beside him I felt reminiscent.

"When I started in my music program, it was all positivity. My mother framed the acceptance letter and my father ordered a blue IC cap for himself from the online school store. My parents came to every performance with hugs and flowers."

"That must have been nice," Jonis remarked.

"At first, I got by. I'm technically well-taught, like most kids who had to practice every night in their living rooms. Have you ever played?" I asked. Jonis shook his head *no*. "I have a firm grasp on theory, which is harder to come by; and the required sight-reading classes, which were a nightmare for most non-vocalists, were easy for me. I held out for a while, but after the praise grew embarrassing I let everyone know that I have pretty refined acute pitch."

Jonis contorted his face into a question mark.

"I hear pitches the way other people see color: I know it without thinking, like you could look at a blue folder and know it as blue," I explained.

"Is it rare?" Jonis asked. "I've never met anyone who could do that before."

"There are levels. I'm AP1, which is a high level and pretty rare. I can pick out every pitch in a complex jazz chord. I can play back or notate a piece I heard through only once or twice."

"I bet the rest of the musicians get jealous. There was this kid I knew in middle school who had a perfectly photographic memory. I hated him."

I giggled with a little snort and looked up at the clock. I had been there for nearly a half-hour already. I felt it was time to jump up and run out the door, but I was heavy and held there to the floor.

"First my peers always tested me," I said. "A lot. 'What's this note, and this one? Sing us an *F sharp*, a *B*... Flatten an *E*, flatten it more, raise it, sharpen it,' and on and on. Before long, I was the most sought-after project partner and an almost full-time after-class tutor. The vocalists always kept an eye on which practice room I was in so they could get me to check their intonation. It was much better hearing from me that they were singing the whole solo slightly sharp, and losing the key at the end, than hearing it the next day from their professors. I attained a sort of fame, which was nice.

"But then we began preparing for our first-year jury: a two-hour performance in front of every faculty member in the program. My professors urged me to 'Feel, express, decrescendo and sfortsando with passion, move your body and mind...'

"They assigned me to take 'The Seasons,' which was my performance piece, and to imagine its landscape: to place each movement. 'What would it look like, feel like at the particular day and moment of the music. Attach it to a memory you have, a memory that you can see and taste and exist in, and use it to fuel the measures into cohesion,' Professor Gove said, her voice going up and up like a chromatic scale. I bet they do things like this for all fields of study, artistic ones at least. What did you major in?" I asked, and then quickly dreaded my assumption.

"History, at Syracuse University," he said, "which isn't as dry as you might think…" I shook my head no, as in *of course it's not dry*, although truthfully I'd never been the slightest bit interested in history. I wasn't obsessed, like other musicians, about how the music came to be the way it was, about the lives and minds of the great, deceased, men and women (well, mostly men) who created an entire world, an entire culture, with sound. I was more impressed with sound in the present, the way life was full of music in every moment, the way sound was always there, constantly coating our experience like air and light. For me, sound was always at the forefront.

"I often imagine that I'm moving through different periods of time, thinking as they thought, feeling as they felt," Jonis continued.

"What time do you like best then?" I asked, expecting to be bored by one of those lectures you get from strangers who want to show you how much they know, how quickly they can unravel the mysteries of the universe before your eyes.

Jonis thought for a moment, then smiled. "I like this time, right now."

It wasn't the answer I had expected. I didn't know how to take it, but when he smiled at me I felt something I hadn't in a long time: desired.

"So, what did you imagine for your music?" Jonis asked.

"There was a mountain range," I said. I readjusted to a cross-legged position to make myself more comfortable, and became acutely aware of my legs, that I could move them so easily, and that the man before me couldn't. "It overlooked the cabin where my family vacationed in the Adirondacks when I was younger. The mountains were beautiful and sloping and expansive and so shockingly green that I couldn't take my eyes off them. There was one mountain that had a round bump on it. My mother and I always called it Nipple Mountain. It was a joke between us before it seemed awkward to joke about such things. 'If you get lost out in the lake, look for the nipple to guide you,' she would say."

I waited to see if he would laugh at me, roll his eyes, to see if he had lost interest yet. His face was patient and difficult to read.

"I would watch Nipple Mountain as the clouds moved across it," I continued. "It never gets boring to watch clouds moving over a mountain, rising, rolling, covering the peaks and then clearing so quickly away. I longed to know what the clouds had said to the mountain. I longed to be close. I watched as the sun reflected off the mountain, paying attention to any new colors that might come out, and to those areas of shade that passed over, black circles of cancerous darkness I couldn't help but be afraid of. The shade was so ominous, and yet every time the spots cleared away to the lush green once again, the mountain mending its beauty.

"I willed upon the sky a giant so vast that he could run his hands over Nipple Mountain and cause it to melt completely away. He had the power to control my mountain with his gentle touch. He had a voice that rumbled like thunder and eyes made of the blue sky, hair of clouds and a body like the blinding glow of sunlight." I paused. "I swear I've never told this to anyone before."

Jonis curved his lips at their ends but did not allow the smile to jump to his cheeks or eyes. "And could you play it," he asked, "the mountain and the giant?"

I pictured myself in the music hall, at the piano bench, on the stage of Ford Hall. My fingers set down gently on the keys as professors and peers sat lady-legged to judge my accomplishments after my one year of study in this program that had and would produce great musicians.

"I thought of my mountain," I told Jonis. "I thought of its strong stance, its crystalline colors, and the movement of my giant caressing the mountain with a desire I wished to someday know.

"I accelerated over the sixteenth runs and I tried so hard to hold myself back. To rock, to push my body, flow through the notes like every glimmering leaf on every tree from my mountain, into the final decrescendo. But my wrists would not loosen and shift and my shoulders could not release. My fingers were stiff and my rhythms at their best moments were robotic; at their worst they were downright wrong.

"I realized on that stage that I have never known that thing which pushes a person from the inside out. In all my years playing I was always aware that what I did could be heard and judged, and because of that it was never truly mine. I love the sounds of the piano. I love its fierce, immovable body. I never loved to perform. I couldn't serve the music in the way I should. I could hear the difference between brilliance and mediocrity. I had known for years which side I stood on. I was never as good a player as I was a listener, and maybe that was my greatest flaw.

"When I stood up from the black baby-grand, I saw Professor Gove's face. Her cheeks turned down like wet leaves." I grabbed at my cheeks and pulled them down to demonstrate. Jonis chuckled. "I felt the energy of completion rush from my body and what came instead was failure – the word alone. I wanted to laugh. A big horrible laugh. I had all of the tools to move the music, but I refused them.

"Professor Gove gave me my evaluation in person the following day. She explained the recommendation that I should pick a concentration that was not performance-based. She told me that my talents would serve me well in the new piano-tuning program. And that was that."

Jonis brought his hands slowly together, holding them tight to each other. His head was down and I urged his eyes to rise. I knew their color, a thing that I could never usually recall about people I was recently acquainted with. I knew they were a shadowy blue. I'm not just adding that *shadowy* in there now; I added the word on that day, *shadowy*, when I thought of his eyes before me. I wondered what he thought of my story. Had I told too much? Had I intrigued him into thinking I was a brilliant human being?

"Ahhhhhhhhhhhh," Jonis sang out suddenly, raising his head. His voice cracked and wavered before it settled on a note. "What's that one?" he asked.

"*E*," I said. "Two points flat."

He motioned to the piano.

"You don't trust me?"

"I want to hear it."

I rose and played him an *E*, and I guessed by the fascination on his face that he had enough musical sense to have recalled his previous note and to know that the *E* on the piano had matched it.

"Ahhhhhhhhhhhhhhhhhhhhhhhh," he sang out, this note lower and more confident.

"*B flat*," I said and then played it on the piano.

He smiled and then let the expression settle. "I bet it gets in the way."

I nodded.

"But it's still remarkable," he said.

I stood up and peered down at him, this strange man spread across the floor in ways I couldn't yet understand. I had to get out of there.

"I know your mother's anxious to get rid of this piano," I said. "I'd love nothing more than for it to be mine, but I have nowhere to put it. I'm sorry. You can sell it if you want, or donate it to one of the schools. I'm really sorry I wasted your time." I turned toward the door.

"Lizzy..."

I turned back to find Jonis crouching on his forearms.

He pressed down with his left knee, grabbed for and pressed into his crutch, and wobbled towards standing. I averted my eyes, afraid he might fall. I looked at the piano, my piano. It would miss me; I knew it would miss me.

"Lizzy, you can keep your piano here for as long as you'd like. I'll make sure nothing happens to it," Jonis said.

He looked at me sadly as he gathered his crutches under his arms. I realized how I might have hurt him, how people may have jumped up and left him struggling his way from the floor before, alone and unable to chase after them.

CHAPTER THREE

In exchange for storing the piano, I had agreed to take Jonis out and around his new little city on Saturday afternoon. Inka, dressed in a red V-neck and tight black jeans, had insisted on coming but refused to provide any help in planning out the events. At the kitchen table I poured over potential activities: lunch, drinks, hiking? No. Not hiking.

"Is he hot?" Inka called to me from the living room, clamping at her hair with a metallic straightener. The chord spread across the room from wall to couch like a hurdle and I had the urge to rise from the kitchen table, to jump it, and to continue right out the door. I hadn't found a way to explain him to her.

"So he's not hot," Inka said conclusively after my silence.

The powdery odor of her burning hair surrounded me like a trap. Inka's hair, like mine, was straight, but she insisted it could get straighter. She pulled the long brown strands through the hot iron again and again with compulsion.

"He *is* good looking…" I said.

"What then?"

"Well, he has a disability."

"Missing an arm? Lazy eye? Tumor on the side of the head? Have you seen the tree man? It's some kind of bacterial thing that makes it look like there is bark growing all over his body…off his hands…there are even leaves!"

I hadn't seen Tree Man and didn't want to.

"Google it later. It's insane," Inka said.

"One of his legs…" I began, but then wasn't sure how to put it. What completed this sentence? One of his legs was different? Was coiled up in a duffel bag? Was long? Was a thing I couldn't name in this world where naming had become so important. "We'll go to Korova," I said. "You'll see when you meet him."

Korova was our bar. It was a clean, narrow space, with white walls, leather couches, and black swivel-chairs at high-top tables. At Korova you could hear your friends talking above the sound of the indie soundtracks or mellow DJs; you could examine the exhibited collections from local artists, which rotated every few weeks so that there was always something new to admire while sipping at your drink or indulging in only slightly overpriced tapas. Inka and I had been going there since we'd turned 21. It wasn't where most of the college kids hung out, but that's why we liked it. We had had our first legal drink upon its sofas, under an odd collection of photographs flipped upside-down and backwards like the world through mirrors while doing a handstand. Since Joe had left for New York, Inka and I had become permanent fixtures there.

Birds were the theme for the current art exhibit. The collection consisted of a series of large canvassed paintings spread throughout the bar. The paintings showed farcical cartoon depictions: a peacock with a handbag about to apply lipstick, a row of colorful lovebirds dressed in suits and ties. There was a long vertical piece that depicted feathers with vivid and varied human eyes at the center of them. It hung to the left of the dartboards, likely the only place it would fit, and I imagined that night must have been a dangerous time for it: the drunken players hurling spears. For now, however, the darts area was empty and the painting unscathed. The twenty or so people who did occupy the bar sat quietly upon the stools and couches having pleasant late-afternoon conversations and, mostly, not staring in Jonis's direction.

"Don't tell me that's him," Inka said, pointing rudely at Jonis who sat at the bar. I pulled her hand down and she giggled, leaned in towards my ear, and whispered, "Freak!"

Jonis's crutches leaned against the bar. His duffel bag had been detached from its sling strap and it rested on the floor with his bundled flesh inside. His pants were long on his deformed side and covered his leg up until the bag took over. There wasn't much of him exposed. All that was apparent from a glance was that he was a man with one leg much longer and a bit wider than the other. Some extra leg, that was all.

I introduced Jonis to Inka and she shook his hand politely. "Really good to meet you," she said like an ambassador. "Welcome to Ithaca. Welcome to Korova!" She ordered Long Island iced teas for all three of us, and took a seat to Jonis's right, the side he was pivoted to face since his leg could certainly not fit if he was turned straight ahead. Inka proceeded to examine him as she sipped at her drink and I took a seat on his left.

"Aren't the paintings cool?" I said to Jonis's back, anxious to break the ice. He turned his head to face me but kept his torso still. His position appeared strained but his face remained relaxed. "My parents have always kept pet parakeets." I continued. "Blue Bird suffered a premature death in our toilet bowl when I was seven…" I paused and waited for the laughter that followed. It always followed. "Now there is Mellow Yellow. He's one of my father's undertakings. My dad feeds and cleans the cage carefully. He lets Mellow Yellow sit and poop on his shoulder. He spends his mornings teaching him to whistle theme songs from 1950s TV shows, and the songs, even off-key as they've been taught, sound gentle. One thing my dad won't do is clip the wings, though; he finds it cruel, so Mellow's always flying about scaring unprepared visitors."

Inka nodded in confirmation of this last part. "He comes out of nowhere," she said with a flapping hand motion. She seemed to be enjoying herself.

"You know, I've been flying in my dreams lately," Jonis told us and it looked to be one of those pieces of a dream that comes in clearly and all at once. "Or more like swinging between trees, but there's that moment in the air when I'm soaring so freely…"

"So you can fly," Inka said, in effect cutting him off. 'No one likes to hear about other people's dreams' was one of her common refrains, and I was thankful that she did not pull it out now. "What else?" she said to sway the subject. "Where are you from? When were you born? What's your story?" Inka looked Jonis in the eyes and nodded. "Yes," she added, "you have lovely eyes."

Jonis turned entirely towards Inka and chuckled. "Well, for the past few years I was living in Syracuse with my college buddy Doug who, as it happens, likes to wear a bird feather in his hair, and I was dating a girl convinced I loved my crutches more than her, and now I'm not; I'm here, twenty-seven, born July sixth, which is also the birthday of the Dalai Lama."

Inka let out a girlish moan. "Wonderful," she said.

Jonis looked in my direction, in order to include me, and caught me amidst an expression of concern. His neck, by now, must have been growing tired from looking back and forth between Inka and me without being able to pivot on the stool. The bar stool must have been tough to balance on with the weight of his leg pulling him down. I was overcome by dread at the discomfort I imagined for him, but there was nothing I could do to assuage it.

Inka, oblivious to empathy, asked for more, asked where he lived now and how he liked it. Jonis talked of the house he was renting on Cayuga Street, and its drastic difference from the 13th-story apartment in Syracuse he had previously lived in. "The elevator life is replaced by the insurmountable narrow stairs life," he said. Inka leaned close to him, flipped her hair in his direction, and only once turned to gauge the reactions of the crowd, to see if anyone she knew might have slipped in, and might now be watching her consort with this odd-looking stranger.

Jonis talked of creaks the house made at night, never in the daytime. Inka was on her third Long Island iced tea and urged me with raised eyebrows to pick up the pace on my (still first) glass.

"There might be ghosts," Inka said. "I've heard of that in these old farm houses. My sister won't live in a house where a person's died. She's obsessed with it. She'll probably get divorced over it. She has her husband and two kids stuffed into this little condo – it's depressing. But anyway, Lizzy tells me you have an office downtown?"

"Technically my mother's," Jonis corrected.

"And what do you do in this office?" Inka asked.

"Take a guess," Jonis replied.

I could smell Jonis's cologne, a rocky-water scent. I felt a tension in my calves, those two bulky muscles where I often sent my stress, causing them to cramp up at times and leave me hunched and smacking. I felt I should have known what Jonis did, but I had been pompous during our last conversation, and had talked only of myself.

"Grad student?" I suggested. I thought it plausible, even likely, that the office belonged to his mother and that he was just accepted at Cornell to study for his master's in one of the new, earthy fields, bioengineering or sustainability, like the type of men who Inka called 'brainy-asses,' and whom she was always finding herself in bed with.

"Grad student isn't a job," Inka said. "What would a grad student need a whole office for?"

I shrugged off Inka's judgments and, for Jonis's sake, hoped that I was wrong. "If you have a better guess, then make it." After I said the words, I regretted them. Inka might suggest he was filming a reality TV show: 'Life with One Leg Too Long.' I didn't put anything past her.

"I was a grad student in Syracuse," Jonis said before Inka had another chance to chime in. "Now I'm helping my mother run her advertising agency: Stark Raving Ads." Jonis paused. Inka cackled. I smiled. "We're a feminist firm. We design pro-women advertising. We also consult for some of the top agencies in the city and help to turn around ad campaigns that objectify and offend women. Many of these said companies are run by men stuck on the idea that the only way to entice women is to show sexy, scantily clad girls, practically orgasming over shampoos and cleaning supplies. It's a new age, and women aren't always responding to these sorts of things anymore. We focus on what this generation's women will respond to. It's no easy task."

When Jonis spoke, his voice struck each pitch assuredly. His words were tonally and contextually pleasing and I responded not to what he said he did or was, not to the reality of the situations he explained, but to the way his words were put forth, the play, the passion behind them. He could have told me he was anything, or anyone, and I'd have thought him perfect.

Jonis took a sip from his drink. He turned to look at a painting of a cardinal perched on the outside of an old-fashioned outhouse with a text bubble coming out of its mouth saying, "Hurry up in there! I gotta go!" He waved to the bartender, Marlo, and asked for another. Marlo came to us slowly. She had thin shiny 30-year-old skin that clung to her face. From behind the bar where Marlo stood, I wondered if she could see Jonis's crutches tilted against the stool, or his leg slung and hanging.

Inka suggested we all do a shot. "You can tell a lot about a person by their preference of shot," she announced. This was Inka's sort of challenge; she rubbed her hands together maniacally and ordered tequila. I requested the only shot which I could take, a lemon drop, foggy and cold and sugary in the way all other shots are not. Jonis looked to me and shrugged as if to ask 'What should I do?' and if I had been able to answer I would have told him to proceed exactly as he did.

"I'll join Inka with the tequila," he said to Marlo and then politely shook her hand and introduced himself, as if to announce that was the first of many times he'd be there. Marlo poured out the tequila, the yellow stream trickling into the glasses, and then mixed a lemon drop both for her and me.

"Cheers," Jonis said, raising his glass. We clinked.

Inka wiped her mouth with the back of her hand like a little kid and spoke her direct word, "Bathroom," which, of course, meant that I was to go with her so we could stand together outside the stalls looking into the mirrors, and talk about Jonis – giggle over his deformity, the silly head tilt he employed when he was thinking.

"I don't have to go," I said boldly, my first transgression. She rolled her eyes and walked away.

Jonis was quiet; he peeked at me and then away. I had a habit of humming when nervous, the droning of my own tune worked to block out the pitches of the world around me. I had to stop myself from doing it, and then moments later, stop myself again. I noticed a stack of blue papers near the edge of the bar and I grabbed for one, held it in my hands. It was about the bird artist: Anthony Wendo.

"The paintings are based on the stories of a woman who believes she was a bird in her past life," I said aloud, reading off the sheet.

Jonis grabbed for a flyer. He read the blurb and then set the paper on the bar.

I looked at the paintings with a new sense of wonder. The bird with the handbag was staring right at me. She was a creamy white peahen with black speckles and sat upon a '50s-style bar stool. Her one fluffy wing drooped painfully from the weight of the handbag strung upon it. Her head was tilted to one side, white tassels popped elegantly like a crown. She reached up with her slender bird leg to apply a bright red lipstick to her beak. This splash of color seemed to bring her pride, to enhance what she was, to satisfy what she was not. That bird in the picture no longer seemed a bird at all, but a woman, every woman, contorting to a new form.

I asked Jonis if he could see it, really see it. He was still glaring down at that paper. He slid it between his fingers, reading it again and again. I thought he might not have heard my questions but then he said "Yes," in a whisper, a sharply pitched *G*. He put his hand on mine. It was a strong hand that did not hold or pat, only lay there. It made my upper arm twitch, but I didn't pull away.

"Wouldn't this just answer everything?" he asked, his hand still upon mine.

He held up the blue paper and it looked bright against the dark wood of the bar. I could see that he had questions burning and I wanted to divert them.

"Did you know that it's considered inappropriate for a Buddhist monk who is aware of his past life to discuss it in public?" Jonis asked.

I shook my head. With Inka's spot at the bar vacant, I worried that someone might stumble up and step on Jonis's leg, not knowing, not expecting it to be there.

"It has to do with their fear of pride, I think. Imagine knowing so much about the world, and not being able to say it," Jonis explained.

"Maybe it's not that simple," I suggested.

"In what way *isn't* it simple? You either share or you withhold." There was a sharpness to Jonis's tone that surprised him into a false apologetic smile; he wasn't used to people disagreeing with him, not so early on.

"What if it can't be expressed? What if words aren't adequate? What if nothing is?" I asked.

"Then how is anyone supposed to learn? There is so much knowledge out there and so many people afraid to share it or to hear it. We are allowed to believe in a God or in a certain kind of science, but everything else is doused in too hard a skepticism to penetrate. I always feel that there is this secret that a few on this planet know and are keeping from the rest of us. Don't you want to know the secret?"

Jonis held up the paper in his hand and shook it in front of me as Inka popped up between us. "What are you all talking about?" she asked.

Jonis's hand jumped from mine. I wondered how long she had been watching us.

"I bet I know," Inka said. "I bet he's finally let out what's wrong with that leg of his and I've missed it all! The most interesting part of the evening!"

Inka patted Jonis on the thigh of his deformed leg and winked at him.

"She's drunk," I said.

Jonis paused his expression, his mouth suspended open and eyes wide, waiting to decide.

"She's sorry," I added, not at all sure that she would comply. I feared she would bring up the tree man.

Instead, Inka leaned in to him, as if she was *really* drunk. She perched her head upon Jonis's shoulder and giggled maniacally. She slurred together some words about the color of his hair, "A lovely autumnly shaaaade." She made like she was about to fall off as she tried to sit back on her bar stool, and she was convincing. I might have believed it but I knew the amount of liquor she could hold and that she was nowhere near her limit. I watched Jonis intently as Inka performed her show. It was better if he thought she was wasted. I wanted him to believe her.

"I was just about to tell a story," Jonis said to Inka. "Would you like to hear it?" He spoke to her as if she were a naughty child, and I admired his condescension; it was something I had not yet been able to muster in response to Inka.

"Yes," she said meekly. She held the bar with her

fingertips and swiveled her hips back and forth on her stool. Maybe she really was trying to behave.

"There was once a little boy named Lhamo Thondup, barely three years old," Jonis began. "There was a party setting out from the Tibetan government in search of the incarnation of the Dalai Lama. From a series of signs, the paths of the searchers and the boy would cross.

"The head of the recently deceased and embalmed Thirteenth Dalai Lama had turned to face northeast, and so this was the direction that the party set off in. Then, a senior lama had a vision upon the waters of the sacred lake Lhamo Lhatso. He dreamt of a three-storied monastery, a path to a hill, a little abode with strangely shaped gutters. And so this is what the searchers set off to find. When the party saw the gnarled sticks of juniper on the roof of a small house on a hill, they went hastily towards it, sure that the Dalai Lama would be inside. To think, if Lhamo Thondup's father had the day before fixed and cleaned the house's gutters, climbed up and swept off the branches, smoothed out the foundation, how things would have been different…

"The holy searchers showed interest in the youngest boy of this destined house. They set out for him a series of possessions that had belonged to the previous Dalai Lama, and then some which did not. Perhaps they lined them up for him like a game. The boy, playing right along, correctly identified each of the objects, saying of those that had belonged to the Dalai Lama – *"It's mine. It's mine."* – as any small child is apt to say.

"With that the strangers acknowledged him to be the new Dalai Lama. He was taken away from his home and his family to a monastery. There was no choice, no explanation, no proper time to say goodbye to the life he had known, a version of his life he would never carry to fruition. His Holiness was to write in a letter some years later in respect to being taken away from his family – *"Now began a somewhat unhappy period of my life…"* He was chosen at a young age to be different, undoubtedly asking, "'Why me? Why me?'"

"A question with no answer," I stated sadly.

Though Jonis said nothing, I could tell by the tuck of his lips in toward his teeth that he didn't agree with me.

"Poor, poor boy, taken from poverty to fame and power," Inka laughed. "I hate these celebrity stories. They depress me."

It was amazing how the three of us could see the same story so differently.

CHAPTER FOUR

I spent the next few days trying to imagine Jonis's life, as if to envision it was to own it. I imagined him driving to work on the busy morning streets, climbing those narrow stairs to the dance studio with the little hint of peril that charged the air around him. I imagined the minutiae of his existence: an elongated bed, a spot in his room to hang his crutches at night, a shower that could in some way accommodate him. I was forced to reflect on this world I was living in, a world with a myth of "normal," and a myth of the entitlement to be so.

By Friday morning, I had run out of restraint. I walked down to the Java Café for an iced coffee; sitting at the long sunny tables in the loft I could see directly into Jonis's office. I covered my face with a beat-up copy of *The Bell Jar*, Plath's only true novel, and watched Jonis leaning over his desk, elbows wide and shoulders relaxed. His face contorted with concentration, a dent between his eyebrows, a tightness in his cheeks. Did I only imagine this dent, this tightness, or did I really see it from my distance across the way? I guess I can't ever say for sure.

Jonis had been the first to arrive at Stark Raving Ads that morning, welcomed only by the whir of the portable air conditioner that hung out towards the street, a droning mechanical sound. He'd cracked the window near his desk open, despite the humid air, to hear the world: wind, cars, the classical music projecting out to the street from the Java, where I sat with my ankles hooked around my tall chair. There was a jungle gym in the middle of the Commons blooming with primary colors, which we could see from our respective windows – it was early but the sweaty children had already begun to stick to the slide, to sway on the swings, to cry out inexplicably.

Jonis conjured his ideas, making lists and sketches. He was writing in a worn spiral notebook with a cartoon cover, the Green Lantern or Ninja Turtles; I couldn't get a clear look. An ad for yogurt, I presumed, since there was a parade of differently sized and packaged yogurt containers that ran across his desk: creamy, smooth, but not, as it has been construed, innately feminine. He swiftly jotted down phrases, syllables, letters, an opening image, a closing idea. He wrote in that quick looping handwriting that I'd not yet grown to know. He filled page after page, flipping them with vigor. It seemed by the flush of his cheeks and the rashness of his arm gestures that he was growing ever more frustrated and less sure. Maybe in a margin my name had found its place, lingering beneath his consciousness.

Like a prelude, a warbler screeched its *tee-zee-tee-zee* from a branch near Jonis's window, and Patty entered the studio. Here, I had my first sight of her, the woman from my answering machine. She zipped across the room and appeared in Jonis's cubicle. Everything about Patty was tight like a rubber band ready to snap, her legs, her arms, her face, her eyes. It made her look older than she was, leathery and seasoned. She said something like, "It's cold in here!" and began to do jumping jacks in a casual way as she and Jonis discussed the doings of the morning. Jonis's expressions were fluid while he talked with his mother; it was apparent how completely and freely he trusted her. I felt envious of this pure composition, as envious as I felt towards the brilliance of Mozart and Mendelssohn, prodigies who could create entire symphonies in their minds as if in concert with the divine. I wanted him to look at me that way.

I had spent more than two hours at the Java. At least two rounds of morning coffee readers had come and gone when a man in an unseasonably thick brown coat sat down beside me. He smelled of salt, body odor, and cigarettes and every few moments he would grunt as if agreeing with an invisible person giving a poignant monologue. As I continued to "read," I instinctively angled myself away from him. I might have been brazen enough to move to another seat, but my view of Jonis would have been lost and things were just starting to get interesting.

Jonis was holding the turquois paper that I had given him the previous weekend at Korova. With the sun shining in onto his desk it looked lighter, almost translucent, but I recognized it all the same. He held it up and examined it thoroughly; the paper connected us.

Jonis reached for his office phone and I watched him participate in what appeared to be a disappointing conversation that I'd later learn went something like this…

"Hi, Anthony Wendo?"

"It is he or is he I?"

"Um? Either way, my name's Jonis. I encountered your artwork at a bar this past weekend and truly admired it. I'm investigating the concept of reincarnation and I was wondering if we might talk sometime about your artwork."

"Ah," said Anthony Wendo. A squeaky note that cracked halfway through. "I don't talk about my art."

"But men with common themes like us," Jonis tried, "might have something to discuss."

"Leave a number if you want, dude. I can pass it on to those of true interest: my subjects, if any of them should choose to call you."

Jonis hesitated, deciding if he should attempt to woo Anthony Wendo any further. It seemed a lost cause. He gave him his number assuming it would never reach a pad of paper, and hung up. It was apparent to me, watching from my distance, that the conversation had gone poorly. Jonis spun his chair around and exited my view for the first time that morning. I worried that the conversation was an omen and that he'd be gone from my sight forever. I cursed the artist Anthony Wendo. The triplet to eighth note of his name – Anthony Wendo, Anthony Wendo, Anthony Wendo – cycled through my mind as I watched Jonis's empty desk for moments that turned to minutes, until I knew that the show was over.

"I am the vermin!" the coated man sitting next to me declared loudly. I wanted to know if he was talking to me or to no one, but I was too afraid to look at him and find out.

"I get one free refill and I'm not going to drink it," I said to him as I gathered my possessions to leave. In retribution for the fear and disgust that he instilled in me, I asked him if he would like my coffee refill. It seemed a fair apology. He grunted and reached out his tattered arm to take my paper cup. I took this as a yes.

From the coffee shop I headed over to Jane's house. Jane lived in Endicott, across the street from my parents. Growing up she had been my neighbor and babysitter. She served as the audience for my amateur musical productions and played student in my games of pretend school. She taught me how to parallel park when my mother was afraid to and my father was unable to because of a lower lumbar problem that wasn't conducive to prolonged sitting. And when I graduated, Jane happily became my first piano tuning client.

Jane sat in her black and silver bar stool at a round table shaped like a peanut pool and set for one. She ticked her foot against the footrest, waiting for me to begin. Her house was eclectic. Certain rooms – the living room, the downstairs bedroom, the office – were stuffy and knick-knacked, having been decorated by Jane's parents who had lived in that house for their entire lives. Other rooms, Jane's bedroom, the dining room where the piano was located, the small sitting room off of the entryway to the house, were adorned with modern furniture and Jane's stark impressionist artwork. The contrast was so blunt that walking from one room to another was a bit maddening.

I started my work in the middle octave with a plan to set each note in perfect relation to the others, like a skilled party host setting name tags on the table in the right arrangement to ensure enjoyable conversation. I thought of my mother before her dinner parties, rearranging flow-ers in a vase, choosing the sharpest knives for the settings of those to which such a thing would matter. Had she always been that way, full of concern? Jane often talked of a different type of woman, a woman before dinner parties, before motherhood. "You're her life now," Jane would add at the end of it, as if I needed this reassurance.

First, each note was set out of tune equally, the temperament process, the dinging of one string and then another. The first octave was the hardest. Madison Comp-ton, the man with whom I apprenticed, would have me tune that first octave again and again. I could hear my mistakes even when Madison could not, and if I had a lot of homework for my other classes, or plans with Inka or Joe, I'd tell him coyly, "I think it's right," and bury that pang of regret in knowing that no one could notice the imperfections of my work but me.

Jane began humming and I asked if she could stop. I had learned over the years that it was better to be rude and let people know when the sounds they were making inter-fered with what I was doing, or were simply irritating me beyond reprieve, since the other option was boiling up in an intolerable rage that it would take me hours to unwind from.

"Oh, sorry. Sorry!" Jane said, surprised that she had

let herself go in such a way. She was usually more sensitive to my "condition."

Once I set that first octave, I began to duplicate the process throughout the piano's other octaves, spreading and creating my balance. Jane's head danced around as I turned the process into a song for her, checking fourths and fifths in a cute pattern of eighth notes. A client once asked me, "With all the technology, how hard could it be to make a piano that could tune up all on its own?" What shook me most was not that such an invention could never treat the tuning of each individual instrument in the way a living ear could, or the fact that a tuning machine would leave me out of a job, but that in those silent readjustments the music of the note not quite right, but getting closer, would be lost.

My mother arrived as I was finishing up. I was playing the "Moonlight Sonata," a piece I knew well. It sounded tonally right; I was satisfied. My mother wrapped her arms around me and I let my hands fall off the keys. She had thick arms, sticky like Ethiopian flatbread, a cool adhesive blanket that you might wrap around yourself to lose the texture of your own skin.

"You've ruined my concert!" Jane said.

"But how about your appetite?" my mother replied, and she dragged us both across the street to my childhood home for lunch.

Inka, who had driven down with me that afternoon, sat at the kitchen table painting her nails.

"I hate that smell," my mother said as she walked in, one arm linked through Jane's like an old lover and the other up and around my hunched shoulders. I pulled away from the chain and caught sight of them still linked together, gravitational opposites – my mother round and mushy, Jane tall and wiry.

Inka finished the last of her nails, the pinky. "I just loved your red – I couldn't help myself," she said and rushed to the kitchen to help my mother carry the lunch plates. Inka was always very helpful at my parents' house.

Jane sat down across from my mother as if this were her place. I took one end and Inka the other. Growing up Jane had joined us for Saturday-night dinners, often with other company as well: friends from work or lonely men who my mother had collected as possible suitors for Jane. But now that I was gone and my parents remained, Jane may have taken to eating with them more often. Twice a week? Three times? I didn't know.

I scooped some chicken salad from a large bowl and made myself a sandwich. I piled on the thick onion slices, awaiting their crisp. My house felt different to me. The dining room was a mess, like my mother had decided to empty everything out of it and then gave up halfway. The house smelled not of recently cooked food or my mother's cinnamon potpourri, but of something bland, dust or air conditioner.

"Lizzy and I entertained a mysterious gentleman the other day," Inka said, and then took a few small pecks of her sandwich. She believed in eating slowly, convinced it helped to keep off weight.

"Are the two of you an escort service now?" my mother asked, pleased.

Inka nodded and I scowled in disapproval.

"He's new to the area," I explained. "We were show-ing him around."

"Suitable for Jane?" my mother inquired. "How old was he?"

"Oh, stop. They don't hang out with men our age," Jane said. "Besides, I've already had three this month."

"Really, Mom!" I said and then shifted my gaze to Jane. "Why do you keep going along?" I asked her.

"Oh, your mother only wants me to be happy. It makes her feel useful."

My mother nodded. "I'm retired in a childless house. Your father is simply no fun. What else do I have to do?"

I shrugged.

"Do you remember Phil?" my mother asked.

I did. He was an old college friend of hers, a man who refused to wear shoes or socks under any circumstances. We didn't see him much in the winter. I wondered if Phil had recently become available or if he always had been. Had any woman desired a man who refused to wear shoes?

"Bare-footed-Phil," I said, an old chorus.

"He loved Jane's paintings," my mom gloated.

"I think what he liked better was to listen to you talk about how much *you* loved my paintings," Jane said. The thought of bare-footed-Phil hitting on my mother made me ill.

In the past, Jane had talked of liking men who my mother set her up with. But the little dates never ripened into affairs. Jane spoke of finding the perfect man and moving with him to a place that was right on the ocean. She talked about these things as boldly and abstractly as she painted. But she had grown up there, in the house where she now lived. She had lived with her parents for her entire life until they each, in their slow way, left her for death. She had been my parents' neighbor upon their arrival in '72. She had driven my mother to the hospital when she went into labor with me and helped my father with the meditative breathing he used to prevent panic-induced asthma as he paced back and forth, awaiting my arrival. She would never leave.

"Stick with Phil," Inka said. "This man we entertained wasn't suitable for anyone. He has this leg.... Tell her, Lizzy."

I didn't want to tell anything about Jonis or his leg, but I couldn't let Inka continue to lead the story.

"He has a deformity. I don't know much about it. It seems one of his legs is much longer than the other one. He walks with crutches. He's a nice guy."

"He had a strange smell. Tell them about the smell," Inka said.

"What?" I asked. There had been no bad smell. Had there?

"Like pizza oil and capers and something else, something raw...fish?"

"What are you talking about?"

"She's touchy," Inka said. "Always looking out for the handicapped."

"Her mother taught her well, then. Forgive the shortcomings," Jane said.

"Or the *long*comings..." Inka added, stretching out the air with her bright red nails. "After Joe it might not be a bad idea for her to aim for someone needy, someone who could never outshine her."

My mother looked at Inka with raised eyebrows and Inka smiled coyly. She should have known better than to mock me in front of my mother.

"Are things a bit rocky with Joe?" my mother asked me.

"They're fine. I just never see him," I replied.

Inka took a large bite of her sandwich and I hoped that it would slow down her metabolism enormously. I hoped that bite of chicken-salad sandwich would tack right on to her neck in a big bulbous bump, irremovable.

CHAPTER FIVE

The walls were round and high, the gray sky a lid, and the rushing falls the stew of some crafty gods. Jonis sat on a flat rock and I beside him piling little stones, seeing how high and how long they could hold. On summer afternoons, like this one, the water was strong. It propelled down and filled everything with its sound. I could find no pitches in the rushing of water, only a peaceful muffled drone.

"The waterfalls are nothing like this in the winter," I told Jonis. "The water levels drop, the falls trickle…"

"Transformation," Jonis said. "Totally fascinating."

We were at a gorge off 96 B. It was a place that Inka and I frequented on hung-over mornings. We would lie on the rocks and let the water glide over us, soothing the headache and nausea induced the night before. There, in the water, I felt no different than the colorful moss, the dirt and bugs, thirsty for existence.

"So tell me more about this bird woman." I scooted forward towards Jonis to hear him better against the gushing water backdrop.

"Well, when Carlotta called me I was shocked. After talking with that asshole artist I had pretty much given up.

I can't believe he actually went to the trouble of giving her my number. I guess some people aren't what they seem."

"I don't know. I think most people are exactly what they seem."

"Carlotta might disagree with you. She's quite a character," he said. "Has these vivid memories of flying and of being covered in peacock feathers. She says she knows the way it feels to birth an egg."

"Would it be much different from birthing a child?" I asked.

Jonis looked perplexed like he hadn't yet considered questioning her story. "Smaller and smoother?"

"Gross!" I said. I placed a final pebble on my little masterpiece of stones and all the rocks tumbled down, scattered as if I had never built anything at all.

"She knows what species she was by the types of feathers that she's seen in her visions," Jonis told me.

"And what species is that?"

"The Black Shoulder Peafowl. Black wings and a gray body. Supposedly the most beautiful of the females."

I thought of the feather spread. I thought of the strut. How could I compare? I hadn't seen Jonis since that night at the bar, and after the way Inka acted I wasn't sure that he would call again. But when he did, I experienced an old kind of excitement, the little girl at a sleepover staying up all night kind. Jonis had been so full of energy: "Oh man, you have to hear what just happened to me! You know that paper you gave me at the bar about that bird artist…" and etcetera. He said I'd be the only one as excited as he was. He said he had to tell me all about it. We made plans to go to the gorge together the next day and I considered the whole thing a ploy – a way to ask me out without really asking me out. But now I was beginning to question this theory. I didn't want to be on a long list of new friends that Jonis called and met up with. I didn't want to be just some part of an idea he was investigating.

"You sound like you'll marry her," I said.

"Well, if you wouldn't mind."

"Why should I mind?"

Jonis laughed. "She must be going on 60. Don't be worried." And I thought: How dare *he* think *I* should be worried? I remember that thought – it was the first time that I judged him by his disability. It frightened me.

"Peacocks have very piercing calls," I said. I recalled their sound as aptly as their shape and color. "*G sharp*, an almost human cry. It's disturbing."

"I have a recording. Want to hear it?" Jonis asked.

"Of peacocks?"

"Of Carlotta."

Before I could answer, Jonis pulled a rectangular tape recorder out from his backpack.

"I didn't know those still existed," I said.

"Maybe they don't. I've had this since the seventh grade."

He pressed the rewind button and that old warbling sound of movement back in time filled my ears.

"It's not too long. She only had a few minutes to talk," Jonis said before pressing play.

"It happened three years ago," the voice on the tape player said. "Glaring into a silver breakfast spoon, of all things. I watched my face curve and bend as I contorted it into various levels of smiles and frowns and realized, suddenly, why I didn't find myself attractive, an issue that had contributed to the low self-esteem I have been burdened with for my entire life."

Carlotta's tone had the forced elegance of a nineteenth century Victorian woman. Her words were carefully prepared, maybe even rehearsed.

"It was not the mole under my chin," she said, "the jagged shape of my eyebrows, or even my pointed nose. I was not pretty because I had no feathers. As simple as that. Right there in my kitchen I had a string of memories, or rather, snapshots: bird's feet, flight, the sensation of a head bob, pecking, feathers, lots of feathers." Carlotta paused.

"The story changes as I tell it. You know that feeling?"

"Yes," said Jonis. His voice was higher and lighter on the recording.

"So I was in the kitchen and I thought of them at first as dreams. But as the flashes continued, over weeks and months, a whole new sensation took over. It was the feeling of identity, something I had never known in this life. I was always floating and then suddenly I had landed. I was once a peahen, I thought. I laughed at the thought. And then I cried at the thought. I researched it next, and then I was sure. Or had I been sure already after the crying and before the research? I have told Anthony Wendo, the bird artist. I have told my therapist, and now I am telling you, and as I say it for the third time now, it is altering still. It becomes a story as I tell it. Does that make me a liar? That is my biggest fear, not of being strange or different, but of being false. It is a conundrum, you see. If I tell family, friends, and acquaintances about what I really am, they will never think of me the same way again. They will not believe me. They will think of me as a kook, a mystic, an old delusional fool. But if I don't tell them, then I really am living a lie. I am pretending to be a woman who is only a woman and nothing more."

"That's a noble fear," Jonis said. He took a pause to smile or avert his eyes or gently pat her shoulder. "When I was young, I dreaded the idea of anyone looking at my leg," he said. "Hospital staff, relatives, friends – the first reaction was always to recoil in horror, to turn their heads or squint in sympathy as if I had just fallen and punctured my leg up in a bloody mess. 'Does it hurt?' they were always asking. Even the covered version, bandaged as I made my way down the street in a wheelchair or on crutches, depending on my health, caused unwanted reactions. People pointed, stared, or worse refused to look at me – staring at the floor or an object behind me in the distance as we talked."

Carlotta moaned as if she knew a similar shame.

"My mother told me I shouldn't hide, that I should be proud of who I was and what I looked like. But the reactions bothered me. They showed, I thought, a complete lack of regard for my feelings. I wondered why, having done nothing to hurt them, these people wanted to hurt me. It wasn't until years later that I took the time to consider what the people around me went through upon seeing me, that perhaps I did cause them a bit of suffering. They felt for me and they didn't know what to do with these feelings. The Dalai Lama believes that man has a natural propensity to empathize with others, a thing in Tibetan called *shen dug ngal wa la mi so pa*, which he believes is reflected in our inability to bear the sight of another's suffering. People look away from me so they don't have to feel and people will shun you so they don't have to think – but might it be our jobs to try and make them?"

There is the sound of fidgeting, of labored breath. "I need to go home now but you can call me. Perhaps our next meeting can be longer," Carlotta said. "You are the kind of man who understands."

Jonis switched the tape off and put it back in his bag to protect it from the heat. The grayness of the day was breaking to a sharp sun and our gazes turned shyly to the ground. I closed my eyes and wondered if Jonis did, too. Since we'd met, I had been observing and piecing him together like a paint-by-numbers, but the colors had mixed so that I no longer knew what shade went where. He had given up too much and now he seemed so distorted.

I opened my eyes and asked, "Do you believe her?"

"I don't know," he said. "I don't think it matters." Jonis wiped the sweat off of his face, up above his hair line, under his eyes, brushing his moon-scar. The heat held tight around us, and when a drop of water splashed from the falls it seemed a miracle.

"How'd you get the scar?"

"Bar fight," he said. "A man smashed a beer bottle over my head." Jonis held an invisible bottle and drew a line with it under my own eye, brushing my skin with his knuckle. I winced with imagined pain.

"Is that the truth?" I asked.

"I can't stand this heat anymore," Jonis said. "Can we swim?"

Jonis shifted his weight around on the rock where we sat and then reached forward. He pulled his leg out of its bag and placed it into one big heap like a deflated hose. It was mummified, wrapped entirely in bandages.

"I wasn't expecting..." I said without thinking.

"This?" he asked, pointing to his leg.

"I mean I didn't even wear a bathing suit."

"What does that matter?"

He began to unwrap his leg from the top down. The revealed skin was a mix of smooth white and rich creamy red. Designs spiraled down his calf and onto the fleshy mass that hung below. His foot was a deeper color; it was puffy and spotted with patches of dried blood. It didn't look like a foot; I wondered if they even called it one. I turned my head in a wince of pain. The tape had warmed me and yet I was still no better than the rest of them.

"There's not much feeling," he said, trying to sooth me.

I placed my finger on his shin and stroked it lightly like the belly of a snake in the zoo.

"Nothing?" I asked.

"Nothing."

Swiftly left and then right, Jonis unzipped his pants down each side, splitting them in two. He revealed teal swimming trunks underneath. The zippers were sewn expertly into the seams so that I hadn't even noticed their clever trick. My black tank-top and underwear would have to suffice as swimwear. I peeled off my jean shorts slowly and Jonis looked at my regular legs, so that I too felt exposed.

I helped Jonis up. We walked into the water and he leaned on me for support. His leg dragged across the ground leaving lines in the dusty rock. With the weight of his body on mine, I was afraid that I would begin to feel sorry for him; instead, I was filled with the suspicion that every girl would fall in love with him if he let them, and I was preemptively jealous of them all.

Jonis looped his hand around my waist as we descended, his long elegant fingers tickled my bare skin. I was afraid that Joe, wherever he was at that moment, could feel me falling away from him, dissipating. We walked deeper and deeper. The water was cold and pulled bumps to my skin. "It feels good to be numb," I said. Jonis may not have heard me, for he had let go of my waist and released himself into the water. He floated on his back, melting into the brown liquid as his leg spread out before us. He was a sculpture; he was an animal, natural and serene; he was a creation from my own mind that had come to life and surpassed my expectations. I ran my hands down his leg to his foot, holding it up so it wouldn't drop to the rocky bottom. His foot couldn't move on its own but the water could make it move; I could make it move. Within my hands I twisted it around in circles.

"What note is that?" Jonis asked me.

It took me a minute to hear the sound of a bird hovering above our heads on a narrow branch.

"*D natural*," I said.

He matched the pitch and used it to say lightly, "What a pretty note."

"Birds are the reason we have music," I told him. I released his foot and made my way up his body, my hands on his shoulders, my legs treading. His face was soft and serene like a fake baby doll. "They made their simple melodies and then we followed."

Jonis nodded, his head bobbed in the water and concentric circles unfurled around him. "You don't think we might have thought of it on our own?" he asked.

"We might have but we didn't."

"Who taught the birds?"

I shrugged. "We can ask your new friend."

Jonis took a breath and fell under the water. He sank down to the flat rocks below us. I thought of saving him, of lifting him up heroically, but instead I watched the way his skin turned gray and then disappeared. I sank down too and let up my breath bubbles as I reached around for him, some flesh of leg or arm to hold, to wait with, until we could rise together.

CHAPTER SIX

Inka was sitting in the living room watching some or other reality show when I got home. The room smelled of her peach-pear hair spray and was sweltering; she was always turning down the air.

"They've stopped playing the 3 o'clock re-runs of *Dawson's Creek*," she said, outraged.

"That sucks."

I took a seat next to her, turned, and straightened my legs out so that they crossed over hers on the couch. I loosened my wet hair from its bun to dry.

"Where've you been all day? I wanted to play Scrabble," Inka said.

"Wanna play now?"

"I don't feel like it anymore."

"Jonis and I went to the gorge."

"Our gorge?" She took hold of my knees awaiting my answer.

"It's the easiest to get to. It's not like I could take him to Six Mile and hike up the canyons, slide down the water-fall."

"Aren't gorges required to have handicapped access-ibility these days? Everything else is."

Inka gave my knees a final pinch and then let go. She adjusted her legs under mine and reached forward for her cocktail on the table.

"Yours is in the fridge," she said. "There are some bands playing downtown tonight. It's supposed to be a beautiful night."

"Are we going?"

"What's Jonis up to tonight?"

"I don't know."

"Well, are you hanging out with him? Are you taking him to our bar and then our park, blyadischa?"

"I forget that one," I said about her Russian condescension.

"Look it up!"

I sighed dramatically and curled my legs back in, away from Inka. "Jonis and I don't have any plans."

"Well then I guess we can go hear those bands."

Four drinks and a hot shower later we stood in the center of the commons. Before us, on a pavilion stage, a local band's drum rhythms and thick electric strumming blared out across the spectator's loud chatter. I wished that I could shush them all, I really did. One thing I hated about concerts was that people would never just shut up and listen, and so the music had to be turned up too loud, distorting the pitches and damaging my ear drums. My head was heavy with the cacophony of noise bending in and away from tonality. I put in my ear plugs, but I still had to stop myself from searching through the notes: *A*, *C sharp*, almost, almost, almost a *G*.

"You all right?" Inka yelled at me. She was part of the trouble, part of the noise.

"I'm fine," I mouthed silently.

Inka started dancing in goofy loops, swiveling her hips and arms. She was wearing a green shirt that made her eyes dark, almost black.

"What are you staring at?" she asked me.

"You look like when we first met," I told her.

Inka threw her head back in a laugh so free it was animal. She pulled me around in a few circles and we danced together for a while until it was all too much and I had to get away.

We stopped inside a long-countered bar where Inka ordered us shots of the best vodka they had. She only drank expensive vodka during the summer when the electric bill was down. She used the fact that she didn't have to pay for heat as an excuse to buy lots of things during the warm season, and I told her she was lucky we didn't live in Florida.

We took three shots. After each one my face folded up and I let out a dreadful squeal that caused the bartender to laugh, though I wished he hadn't.

"Some girls can't handle their drink," Inka called to him over the '90s pop song playing. The chromatic female vocals rose up to a dramatic top.

"He likes me," Inka said too loudly, too confidently, and as if in response he handed her a coaster with his name, Carl, scribbled in a half-script, half-print score, followed by his number.

Inka took the emblem of his desire with a smile, hooked her arm in mine, and marched us out of the bar. I enjoyed being guided, her body an extension of my own as our clunky two-headed being staggered along. We walked into the crowd of fuzzy unfamiliar faces and I spotted a group of boys, certainly college boys, probably sophomores who'd rented a house for the summer, looking toward us. Inka pulled me over to them and before I had any time to think I had my hands upon the chest of a tall boy to stop myself from falling into him. He looked down on me from an octagonal face with far-spread eyes and a small sweet nose. He looked down like he knew me and I felt I had stepped into somebody else's reality, somebody else's life. I couldn't find the heart to say to him, "You are a stranger. You are nobody." So, while the bands played, one after another, that octagonal boy and I may have exchanged words about the state of our country, we may have discussed *The Elephant Show*, and we may have kissed a series of long warm kisses. None of it mattered but that he looked at me like he wanted me, and I wanted him to keep looking. I felt a part of my generation for the first time in a long time, a generation where religion, science, and philosophy alike had been replaced by an obsession with lust, by a belief that catharsis, happiness, and truth lay only in the jittery euphoria of desire; it was all that we could believe in.

Before long Inka pulled me violently away from the boy, to a side alley. I thought she was going to give me a lecture on fidelity or threaten to blackmail me with a photo snapped of that boy and me in sloppy action. She'd hold it before Joe as proof that he should forget me once and for all.

"What?" I asked her. "What's wrong?"

"I had the most embarrassing moment of my life!" Inka filled her face with color and dramatics; I wondered why she had never tried acting. I crossed my legs at the ankles and took a seat on the cool ground, feeling unable to balance myself properly.

"I was flirting with this one guy, Sean, and we were dancing—he was a good dancer too; he had good hips—and then his friend came over and handed him a cigarette and I turned to look at the friend and asked if I could bum one, and as he turned to me I realized that he's this guy I slept with like a month ago after we went to the bar that one night and did the ab-feeling contest. He looked at me for a minute and then recognized me and said to Sean, 'I've already done that one.' Oh bozhe moi, it was mortifying. God. Oh God. Wait here!"

I stayed on the ground, my back against a brick building, while the sound from the concert came in heartbeat pulses. I let my eyes close and pretended to sit at Mrs. Malburn's piano. I spread my fingers and played something I imagined to be melodic and spectacular. With my imaginary piano in front of me, all the noise around me felt alive. It reminded me of my days as a music major, before I ever knew I could fail. Those late nights in music halls full of young musicians whose energy was so strong that it seeped under the doors of the practice rooms and infused my fingers. A time of possibility. A time of hope. I could have captured those passions, my own and the others', ingested them to keep. I threw my head back and allowed my fingers a long jazzy run on the air in front of me. I must have looked crazy but when Inka returned she didn't notice. "Here!" she said. I opened my eyes and dropped my hands. Beside Inka stood the boy who I might have talked to and might have kissed. "You two look good together." She winked.

The boy reached down for my hand and I let him pull me up. His skin felt dry and sad.

"You need some lotion," I said to him. "I want to go home."

Inka frowned dramatically and pointed to the boy. "I brought him back for you. I risked being seen again by Sean!"

"Please, Inka, I need to go home."

Inka shooed the boy away, grabbed my hand and started running through the crowded streets, dragging me along. "Want to play hide-and-go-seek?" Inka asked.

"If I hide you'll never find me," I said.

I ran into a parking lot and ducked to the side of a rusted Dodge truck. Inka retrieved me quickly; she could hear my breath and my laughter. Tired from running, we sat down on the ground in front of a minivan.

"You know I've been rooting for you and Joe," Inka said. "But I can see he's disappointed you. I want you to know, Lizzy, we can find you someone better, someone grand! Carl has a friend…I showed him your picture and he wants to meet you."

I frowned, wished desperately that I had some water, thought of all the things that I would sacrifice to have even one sip of cold water: my earrings, my shoes, the cheap ring on my left hand that I got at a flea market, my right eyebrow that always curved up too jaggedly.

"But you can't date that disabled man, Lizzy. I won't let you. Can you hear me, Lizzy? Are you sober enough to remember? You'll never be normal after a thing like that. You won't recover!"

She stood up quickly and took off. I hurried after her.

"Weeeeeeeeeeeeeeeeeeeeeeeeeeeeeeeeeeeee," she called out as she ran up the street towards our house. The note was shrill and sharp, a bird's sound. I followed her until I was too tired to run anymore. I had nearly caught up when I felt a bump from the inside of my head, someone knocking. "You all right?" Inka asked, turning back to me. I heaved forward and threw up on the ground, missing Inka's right foot by an inch.

CHAPTER SEVEN

Hungover and disoriented from the night before, I received an uncharacteristic early morning call from my father. He wanted to meet me for breakfast, but when I explained that I didn't feel well, he settled for lunch.

We met at my father's favorite diner, where he'd eaten breakfast alone at precisely 7 AM for as long as I could remember. He wore his tweed jacket, which he'd sewn himself when I was eight or nine. I recall him as a slow meticulous sewer. His projects extended on and on, some never coming to an end. The jacket was completed, finally, after a year. When he wore it out for the first time, to dinner in downtown Endicott, I asked him if he could make me one exactly like his. He laughed. I waited for months, through eight nights of Chanukah, but my jacket never arrived.

Across the table from me, now, this jacket looked stifling. My father rubbed its patchy elbows. Perhaps he'd grown heavier and it no longer fit correctly. He ordered a salad and picked at the greens. We never had lunch like this, just the two of us, without my mother. My grilled-cheese sandwich looked colossal, thick sourdough bread and fluffy yellow cheese. They use too much cheese at diners. Too much everything. I couldn't imagine ingesting it but I tried with small bites, picking the sandwich up and then putting it down again between each one.

"Your mother's kicked me out of the bedroom," he said, pushing around a tomato. He didn't look me in the eye and I couldn't remember if he ever had. What color were my father's eyes? I knew they were green-brown, but I couldn't conjure the shade, maybe ocean, maybe olive. I didn't even know.

"She comes home late. Eleven. Twelve. Sometimes one. She won't talk about it." He shook his head. "She tells me to be patient. I'm not supposed to be telling you."

My father rubbed his bald shiny head with both of his hands, then reached into his pocket for his black tube of chapstick, the same kind he'd been applying all my life. He waited for my response.

I thought for long, too long. My father started munching on some cucumbers. I was flooded with strange excuses. You snore loudly. She's having night sweats again. I wanted badly to explain to him something he had not considered. I wanted him to go back to being my father, the one who would not be sitting here with his daughter at a diner, having this conversation.

"Have you asked her what the problem is? What you can do?" I said finally.

He did not blush or wince, only nodded his head 'yes,' and then shook it again more slowly.

"I'm a silly old man," he said. "I'm sure it's part my fault. And I'm really sorry to burden you but what should I do? After thirty years what does a person do?"

It took every effort for me not to cry ridiculously in that diner for anyone to see. I knew how much he loved her, not in the ways of lust or endearment, but in a permanent way, the way he loved me. I thought of my mother, her face, her voice; it turned sour until she was nothing that she had been, a distorted green oblong ache. Some unrestrained tears escaped from my face.

"I'm sorry," my father said. "It's fine. You know it's fine. I shouldn't have said anything but I didn't know what to do. What does a person do? What does a person do?"

I hated when he repeated himself. I thought he might be crazy. He might be feeble. Did he think that I could answer him? That I could fix this?

"You try," I whispered. "Make a time. A date. Dinner at 5. Movies at 7. She won't say no. She'll come home for you." As I said these words I thoroughly believed that she could love him again, that she would have to. And when I finished saying them, in the silence that ensued, I knew that I was wrong.

"I'm trying," my father said. "I'll try."

He shoved a large leaf in his mouth and seemed to swallow it whole.

"That Jane, she's nice and all but she's always there. She eats with us every night your mother is home. And then they go off together to Jane's house to watch some or other TV show and your mother returns all giggling and wined up and too tired to talk to me. She says she has run out of things to say. I know I'm not the most interesting man, Lizzy, but I'm all alone over there. I shouldn't have to be all alone."

I nodded. He was right. He was a good man, but what did that matter? I wanted to tell him that we all end up alone and sad and wishing for something more. I wanted to tell him to get a dog, but there was the problem of his allergies. I had nothing to say. I took a bite of my grilled cheese and the soft milky gush between my teeth made me gag. We finished the meal in relative silence. After we received the tacky mini clipboard with the bill and before the receipt from my dad's card was signed, I kissed my sad father goodbye on the forehead and walked out alone claiming I had an appointment to make it to.

From the diner I started out on a walk towards the Java for some hot tea to calm me, but soon found that I'd passed the café without noticing. So I continued down the main road, by the rows of organized houses with elaborate trendy gardens blossoming out front. I turned up a hill because it appealed to me. Round like a man's belly, it was a hill that wore its pavement out; cracked and potholed, the hill kept outgrowing it. I was on the sunny side of the street, and my eyes squinted to fight to the light, but I would not shut them. I watched the road seams, the bottoms of trees, my feet with their steady ba-dum ba-dum. I felt a pull to the ground so that if I had wanted to jump I couldn't have. The road held me to it and I could not escape.

Inside my mind the thoughts were growing loud; they had pitches of their own, not just a ringing tinnitus but identifiable notes, chromatic consonants and vowels climbing up. The words were soon lost to pitches altogether, rising with high tonics and dropping down to darker, more dissonant bass thwacks that hardly vibrated at all. I felt congested and unable to clear anything out. My fears and problems were unsolvable musical equations. Could you call them compositions? They were complex enough to have involved a whole orchestra, but they were not memorable, not beautiful, nothing I cared to notate. I imagined that musical virtuosos might have had minds that worked in ways similar to mine, only I couldn't turn it, any of it. I lacked art and had only mechanics. I couldn't choose the pieces properly or figure a way to arrange them. The noise inside me was heinous in its chaos like I imagined hell to be, a thing void of selection where color, sound, stench, and soul were thrown into piles neglected and unloved, a world without culture, without art, without the essential concept of beauty from which these things emerge. I closed my eyes and breathed, loud windy breaths whirring in and out; I wanted to be silenced.

The outside sounds emerged softly. Birdsongs intermingling in the air with a pause to listen and respond. The inharmonic chimes hung on a farmhouse porch. The lilting melody of a radio. The long, irregular oscillations of

un-pitched noises: the shuffle of my own feet, the foot-
steps of a man ahead of me on the road who scurried then
paused only to scurry again, the banging of a hammer in
the distance, the wind, the rush of passing cars – wheels
against pavement and metal against air. I imagined the
vehicle of these noises, unlike the noises in my mind that
started and ended too close to their source, the outside
sounds had space, time, waveforms of different shapes and
sizes, invisible curves inches or feet long. There must have
existed, in that moment, a wave the same size as Jonis's
leg, and how I wanted to know what sound it was making.
How I wanted to see it dance with the air, with the other
sounds, exploring its impact until all of the energy had run
out.

I was pulled fully back into the world by the presence
of another, the man who had been shuffling up ahead of
me. I slowed my steps awkwardly to prevent myself from
catching up with him, annoyed that the world was so
peopled that one could not be alone even when they had
wandered far out of town, over hills and down country
roads. He wore faded jeans and had his long blond dreadlocks pulled back in a tie, certainly part of the large crew of
town hippies. I dreaded the impact of being seen by him,
of becoming a thing outside my mind, observable.

I was walking as slowly as I could, thought of turning
around but was compelled by forward momentum, when
he stopped near a yard strewn with used automobiles and
headed for the blue house that sat on the property. I
paused by a tree and ran my palms over the rough bark. I
untied and then re-tied my shoes, slowly, repetitively, so
that if the man had turned around I would have seemed
busy and would not have appeared to be stalking him. The
man walked up to the furthermost window of the house
and stopped. I had no illusions that he was the owner of
this house or that he knew anyone inside. He adjusted the
bag on his back, a faded green sack covered in colorful
patches that I was too far away to read but I assumed were

all different clever ways of saying that people and animals and the world should be free. The man leaned forward, cupping his eyes so that he could see into the house, and I noticed a hole in his jeans underneath the left back pocket, a tethered window that revealed his flesh underneath. He turned his head abruptly checking around him and I ducked behind the tree. He looked up towards the sky with a slow longing; I was sure he was praying for forgiveness and in that moment I became afraid of him. What would I do if he were to break into that window he was peeping through? If he were to steal a flat-screen TV or a reclining chair? Would I chase him down the street as he lumbered with the large objects? Would I tackle him to the ground and cry out, *Help! Thief!* Would anyone respond to my calls? Would I stand face-to-face with him and ask, *Why do you do it?* Would he answer, *It's a lonely life and we all go around doing things. One thing after another. Whatever we do ends up hurting someone…?*

The man looked away from the sky and crouched down to the ground. He pulled something out of the bag on his back and started fiddling with it. I backed away slowly though I feared that he already knew I was there. I put my pocketbook over my chest like a shield as I tiptoed further back, creeping behind one tree, then the next. I tried not to crunch on the twigs beneath my feet. I tried not to breathe.

The man raised his weapon toward the house, aiming it right at the window. I worried it was a child's room, worried that it was anybody's room and that they might be in there having an afternoon nap and that I might be witnessing the last moments of their life as I retreated like a coward. I wondered what the person inside that house had done to call this perpetrator on. It would be better if it wasn't random, I decided, if there was fight, a mistreated sibling, a cheated on wife, a long childhood argument never resolved. It would always be better than a random act of violence, unexpected and inexplicable.

I thought of my own home, a place now destroyed. It may as well have been robbed, ransacked, pillaged, shot to pieces, burned from the inside – for suddenly it was devoid of the permanence that had been its best quality. It had been emptied of the loving family that had once occupied it and now two lonely people lived there unable to amuse or console each other. I knew where everything was – the snack drawer, the towel closet, the penguin figurines perched on a pond – and yet I knew nothing, my parents no longer in love, no longer lovers, and though I'd never wanted to think of them having sex, the thought now that they didn't, couldn't, wouldn't, felt shattering. The unity that had created me was now destroyed. With one misstep, I too could be destroyed.

The man held the gun pointed at the window but then quite unexpectedly he dropped it back down to his side and looked up toward a tree where a red-bellied robin sang a Beethoven melody in *C*. I concentrated on the music, allowed it to calm me. This could be my chance. He was distracted; I could turn and run away. He was scrawny, underfed, deranged … he wouldn't catch me. I took a breath but as I was about to run he raised the weapon to eye level again, pointed it right at the window. I couldn't let it happen.

"Noooooooooo!" I screamed.

Before I could run forward and launch my attack, the man fell backwards in surprise and dropped on the ground what I saw to be a camera rather than the gun I had taken it for, a cumbersome black camera.

I moved towards him in amazement. I should have been relieved, but honestly I felt more afraid in that moment than I had ever been in my life. I had realized insanity.

"What's going on?" the man asked from the ground. He looked up to the tree where the robin had been.

I didn't answer. What could I say? I kept walking towards him as if my movement alone were an apology or an explanation.

"You should have seen this shot I had: the bird was reflected in the window. You could see the interior of the room and the tree and the bird outside, as if the two worlds were one. Damn it. It's gone now," he said not necessarily to me, though I was the only one who could hear him.

He picked up his camera and stood. He started walking towards me.

"Hey, I know you," he said. "You live across from the old abandoned house on Columbia. I took some photos there a few weeks ago, had to crack up some of the windows first. I was afraid you and your friend might call the cops on me or something."

"Yeah," I said. "You were cracking up the windows."

"I'm working on a reflections series. Man, I wish I had gotten this shot."

I started to cry, my arms hung down. I didn't even try to hide myself.

"It's okay, kid. There's nothing to cry about. There'll be more birds reflected in windows. It's only a matter of careful searching."

I cried harder and the man put his hand on my head, his palm spread out and the weight of his arm pushed down like he wanted to send me through the ground. Then he lifted his hand quickly, the pressure releasing in a sudden burst. I felt myself stretch up, rise towards the sky.

"Relax," he said.

"We thought you were drunk that day, when you were throwing stones at the window. I'm sorry. We did almost call the cops," I said.

"I *was* a little drunk."

That made me laugh. I finally let my hands up to assist my face by wiping away the snot and tears.

"I'm going to go back to taking pictures now," he said. "Will you be all right?"

I nodded.

The man adjusted his zoom and photographed a little bird that had landed near our feet. He click-clicked his camera to the bird's tune. I wanted to thank this man for caring to follow and photograph a singing bird reflected in a window, to thank him for carrying a camera instead of a gun, to thank him for sparing my life. Instead, I turned and ran until my breathing was too heavy and I could not run anymore. I grabbed my cell phone out of my car and saw that I had a voice message from Joe, a rather startling song, which he must have recorded on my machine the previous night.

"Stop! In the name of love. Before you break my heart. Think it o-o-ver."

His voice was sleepily languid and I played it over three times.

CHAPTER EIGHT

I had been introduced to Joe five years earlier, during our first month of college. It was a hot afternoon and after my morning classes I had an idea to build a slip-and-slide out of garbage bags on the sloping field outside our dorm room.

"The hill is ours," Inka declared with a swoop of her arms. I backed away, afraid of being accidentally struck. I was still getting used to her.

"If there were more people setting it up with us I'd feel better. What if we do the whole thing and nobody shows?"

"We're here. What else matters?" Inka said.

She squeezed my shoulders and smiled. I had been falling for her since we first met.

By the time I arrived at my dorm on that first day, the room already smelled of Inka: a sharp perfume by Ralph Lauren and the almond butter odor of her wrinkle reducing cow's milk lotion. She was alone, carefully unpacking her boxes, and I felt unreasonably childish with my parents lugging in my things and helping me arrange them. My parents and I traveled up and down the one flight of stairs together asking inconsequential questions: "Did you see the box with the towels in it? Did you forget to bring the new comforter Aunty Nora bought you?" My mother lapsed into bouts of crying, tears pouring down her face, but she carried on with the unpacking and regular conversation as if she wasn't leaking at all. I was so much a part of my small family that it was embarrassing. "It will be so quiet without you," my father kept saying. I didn't take the time to imagine the silence, the house devoid of my and my mother's constant bickering and laughter, my and my father's games of Boggle: clinking letter-dice and the sound of the piano – gone. I thought only of the new life: the stress of classes starting, the chaos of my belongings stuffed into that small room, and my roommate who I was sure must have regretted me already.

Not a month later, Inka and I had formed our own sort of family. I straddled the window ledge of our first-floor room, one leg hanging next to Inka's bed and the other dangling outside, a few feet up from the grass where Inka stood. I handed her the buckets full of sudsy water that we had filled and lugged down the hall from the bathrooms while Inka sang loudly, her scratchy voice jumping pitches faster than I could catch them. I thought of splashing water on her but wasn't sure how she might respond, so I handed the buckets carefully, threw down the box of high durability garbage bags that Inka had stolen from the dining hall, and then jumped out. We fastened the bags together with a roll of red masking tape and spread our track down the hill, twenty garbage bags long.

"Long enough?" Inka asked.

"I think so. I'm trying to remember what it's supposed to look like. I had a bright blue slip and slide with an inflated little pool decorated with hippos at the end."

"And a one-piece suit in sparkly orange, I assume." Inka said. "Oh, the '90s."

We attached a few bags in a large square at the end of the slide for landing and walked back up the hill.

"Take off your damn clothes," Inka yelled at me

when we reached the top. I checked to see if anyone else could hear her. No one was close enough. "I don't want to be the only one in a bathing suit. People will think I'm extroverted," she said.

"You are," I said.

I took off my tank top and before I could become insecure about my glowing white stomach or the small ring of acne scars on my back, we were surrounded by a crowd of kids fresh from class, tearing off their clothes and throwing themselves down our sudsy hill. They were gorgeous with their spontaneity and I loved them all.

"More water," Inka yelled, and I was glad to be in charge of retrieving buckets-full from our dorm and pouring them down the slide. Inka began to call me the Water Goddess and suddenly I had taken control of the crowd, putting people in line and deciding when the slide was or wasn't appropriately moistened.

Around noon, a boy approached our slip and slide wearing only a backpack and khaki shorts. I didn't know his name, but I recalled his eyes. As a freshman piano major I was required to put in time playing at rehearsals for the various choral groups on campus. During one choir rehearsal as I played perfect arpeggios for our warm-up, and then struggled through a sight-read of Leonard Bernstein's "Adonai," this same boy that stood before me now had glided reluctantly around the piano, glancing up at me with an embarrassed smile.

In the Ithaca College choir they practiced Dalcroze, a method of learning music through movement. At this particular rehearsal they had been working on phrase — stepping the beat across the acoustic room as they moved their arms forward and then back according to the appropriate phrasing of each line. Joe was the only freshman in this touring choir, everyone knew about him; it didn't happen often that a freshman was given such an honor. He splayed his fingers open and pushed his arms back and forth like the most ungraceful dancer. He stared at a spot on the floor, avoiding eye contact with any of the upper-classmen who laughed and smiled freely, having become accustomed to such exercises and maybe even appreciative of their usefulness. Joe was among singers who would go on to get their Master's at Julliard or tour Africa learning styles of indigenous singing to bring back to elite music workshops. He would go on tour with them in Germany in just a few months. When I'd heard of him, I was immediately jealous of this prodigy. But when I saw him dance that day with his awkward bulky muscles and the pain of embarrassment on his face, I felt only longing. I gave him a sympathetic smile and caught his eyes, green and gleaming as if he may have been crying or might cry sometime soon. And now he stood before me on the hill.

"Hey, Inka, what do you have going on here?" he asked.

Inka lifted her chin and I noticed a mole in the center of that fleshy triangle between bones.

"Where's your shirt?" She thrust her chest at him provocatively.

"Oh, I left it down by the practice rooms. I'll go back for it tomorrow. It's so freakin' hot!"

"Tell me about it. We built this slip and slide – more of a turnout than we expected."

"Great day for it!"

I don't know what came over me but I took off with a run, belly first. I held my hands beneath my shoulders and the back of my thighs curved up for everyone to watch. There was a thick line between my arched shoulder blades where my hair gathered together, wet and sticky, down into the gap. I pictured my body the way he might see me, and I liked it. I spun out at the bottom gracefully and scrambled quickly out of the way as another girl from the crowd took a high jump onto her backside and began down the slide, pushing her hands along the grass to increase her speed.

"You want to try?" Inka asked Joe.

"Sure. Why not?" he said.

He threw down his bag and walked slowly to the track.

"Let me add some water," I said. I wanted to protect him. I brushed past his right shoulder and hurled a bucketful as he watched me.

"We're in English together," Inka said to me. "This is Joe," she pointed at him. "And this is my roommate Lizzy," she pointed at me.

"Yeah, we've seen each other before," Joe said.

I was thrilled that he had remembered. Joe made a dramatic motion with his arms to mock himself and his dancing Dalcroze. He reached up to give first me and then Inka a high-five.

"The slope's all yours," I said, flipping my hair.

He took off with a run and a lovely C-pitched whoop that echoed across the grassy fields where students walked, chatted, and laughed. It echoed from the towering dorm rooms to the expansive dining hall, across the lawn strewn with young bodies enchanted by sun and by the newness of freedom that had unveiled itself before them. It was a sound to symbolize my new life, while twenty miles south, there was another new sound carrying through the home I had left – a deafening silence.

Movement II

In your loneliness do not look at the road,
And do not rush out after the troika.
Suppress at once and forever
The fear of longing in your heart.

Nikolay Nekrasov ("Troika")

CHAPTER NINE

The peacock is a boastful creature, carrying an elaborate spread of feathered eyes that hold it down to earth, so that unlike other birds, the peacock cannot fly higher than fifteen feet or for longer than a few minutes. The peacock is like a woman wearing a tight dress and stiletto heels: all for show. It's like those flowers that bloom in bright pink or teal, colors that seem made up by clothing stores for the summer season, burdened by beauty and always the first one picked.

Carlotta sat cross-legged under the shade of an evergreen near the water's edge at Cayuga Lake State Park. Wrapped in an oversized teal cardigan, she drank from a metal canister and focused on this act as if it were a challenging one. Her clunky red-framed glasses appropriately hid her beady blue eyes, though the scattered hairs of her short blond cut did nothing to distract from her overwhelmingly shiny forehead. I was both surprised and a bit relieved that she wasn't beautiful. As we approached she waved us over and then avoided eye contact by sipping. When we sat down, her hand jolted and she spilled all down her chin onto her sweater and wiped it away with the back of her hand in an elaborate swoop. The world was fading to muted yellows, burnt oranges, and browns below, beneath, and around us; but Carlotta and the evergreen that rose behind her were full of refreshing color.

"You have the long arms of a dancer," Carlotta said to me and then I remembered the elegance of her voice from the recording, the harmonic rise and fall, the assured end of phrase that perfectly juxtaposed her sloppy appearance, making her a more complex and multifaceted creation than I had expected. I crossed my arms, now feeling them as conspicuous monkey limbs. I was expecting Carlotta to be an elaborate farce, a dramatic and attention-hungry liar, and now that I was here with her I wasn't so sure.

"Jonis has told me that you have a talent for pitch," she said. "It's important to have a talent for something."

The breeze off the lake whirred in D through the muted grey of the sun, the parched fall air.

"Oh, it's not a talent, really," I said. "Nothing I've had to work for. I was pretty much born feeling pitches as distinct; as soon as I knew the names of the notes, then I could pick out which notes belonged to which names. We can all categorize colors, sights, types of sounds ... I only have an additional category: pitches." This was a speech I had given before.

"It is, by definition, a talent," Carlotta said decisively. "Perhaps we would all have it if we lived in a differently constructed world. Perhaps we would all know which note was which, where we came from, and where we are headed. These things are inside of us and why shouldn't we be able to know them, to access them? We learn to be blind."

Jonis nodded in agreement, he looked at her with the wonderment of a disciple to his guru.

"I'd really like to believe that the answers are somewhere inside of us, but..." I started.

"It is not a matter of belief," Carlotta cut in. "It is a matter of composition. We have the ability to arrange everything: our days, our ideas, our language, our beliefs, our senses and responses to those senses. There is a massive societal symphony that we are participating in all the time." Carlotta looked at me. Her face was asymmetrical, all features tilting to the left. Her ears stuck out like wings, which might spread out and take off. "It is everywhere. I know you can hear it. We are all playing along, but very few of us have the strength to pull back, to step away for long enough to compose something new."

Jonis fidgeted his hips into the earth, adjusted his leg and checked on his neatly piled crutches. I was beginning to feel that this was some sort of test or indoctrination. Carlotta introduced the material and Jonis sat waiting to see how I would respond.

"I don't know," I said. "Nowadays everyone thinks they're an artist. Everyone's a writer or an actress or a musician. Everyone goes to liberal arts colleges and has a blog and is in a band. We're all writing history."

Carlotta didn't wait a beat to disagree. "They are playing along," she said, "bowing their mediocre melodies. It doesn't matter if someone *thinks* they are an artist, one either is or is not. An artist perceives the world in a new way, in a way different from what they were taught; anyone else is an imposter."

I was overtaken by a chill. Jonis took off his jacket and handed it over to me. I tried to object but he wouldn't have it. "This is my favorite time of the year," he said. "I love to feel *cool*."

Both Carlotta and I laughed. I wished I could suggest that we walk. Some conversations are meant for walking, for the world transitioning around you, the blood pumping through the body rather than pooling idly.

"I should have brought some snacks," Carlotta said. "I am never thinking ahead." Her hands were tense, jittery, as she took another sip from her canister. She turned to look at a flock of ducks that floated by tiredly and her self-assured voice fell away to her apprehensive demeanor.

"I envy them," she said of the ducks. "Together and knowing what they are. You see, when I turned 34, as Jonis may have told you, I became inundated with flashes of memories, dreams, scents, sensations from another life, the life of a peacock. As sudden as the realization was, it retroactively explained oddities, insecurities, and desires I had felt throughout my life. I felt a missing piece had been found. I thought, "Aha!" and things fell into place. For whatever reason, I could see the world and my life more clearly."

Carlotta pulled off her glasses to clean with the edge of her shirt. In cleaning, she exposed her stomach briefly, a slouching wrinkled collection of skin. It felt too intimate to look at and I averted my eyes.

"When Jonis told me about you, about your abilities, I thought you might be able to help me," she said.

"Help you?" I asked.

"In finding some proof," she said.

I had been aware that Jonis had wanted me to see if there was any correlation between her voice, pitches, patterns, tones, and the calls of a peacock, but I hadn't known that he had told her about it. I thought that he was the one questioning and looking to believe in her in order to satisfy some sense of purpose in his own life, some answer to that question he had asked me that first night in Korova: "Why me?" Carlotta asking for me to help her believe in herself was an entirely different matter – one I wasn't prepared to face.

"I'm no artist," I said. "I'll openly admit that. I'm not composing anything. I have no expertise. I don't think I'll be able to help you."

"Now Jonis says you are not the type who believes in things…"

"Oh, does he?" I asked.

Jonis looked meek.

"I am not asking you to believe," she said. "I do not even 'believe' myself, per se. I acknowledge that this whole thing might be a reaction to stasis. I was unsure of my purpose, of my true identity, and so I may have, unconsciously and as a survival mechanism, created the illusion of a new sense – the sense of a past life.

"This is to say," she continued, "that we each create our own identity, and are always in the act of creating it for as long as we live. Perhaps even before we lived and then again after. We may always have been in this act of creation."

Carlotta reached out and placed her hand on my forearm. She gave me a pat.

"I'm talking too much. I'm always talking too much. Don't you worry about it."

I wasn't sure what I wasn't supposed to worry about, which caused me some worry.

Carlotta shifted her gaze to Jonis. "What do you have?" she asked. "We didn't get to that before."

For a moment I didn't know what she meant.

"Malfunctioning KTS gene," Jonis said. "It means there are abnormal blood vessels which damage the tissue, causing a reverse blood flow where blood is coming back into the tissue instead of being cycled out with all its toxins. Then, the body tries to cut off the abnormal blood flow with rapid growth, hence the leg. One wrong signal that the body tries to correct in all the wrong ways, constantly fighting itself. Maybe that's what bodies are always doing, only in mine one side always wins and the other always loses. The balance is wrong."

On the rare occasions when Jonis discussed his disease, he explained the whole thing so concisely. I loved the confidence in his wording. The way Jonis described it, it was hard to believe that all bodies didn't have similar problems and confusions, wrong turns on the blood flow highways, and then the moment of panic when the mistake must be corrected, over-steering straight into the guardrail.

"How do they treat it?" Carlotta asked.

"They don't, really. Or that's what my mother is

always complaining about. She has these theories about correcting the body's actual processes, teaching it how to route the blood, to stop the hypertension, healing through re-education; it's similar, strangely, to her theories on international conflict. So far, though, she hasn't become a scientist or a general. For now, they remove parts of tumors if they think they have the potential to become cancerous or if they're threatening a vital organ. They treat the varicose veins, they give me different materials to wrap the leg in to provide support and comfort, different medicines to prevent infections on the skin, and blood thinners. Mostly they amputate."

"Isn't that the way of this world?" Carlotta said. "Eliminate anything that can't be understood."

The breeze began to change as the sun set, a deep unidentifiable whir.

"I'm coming by a premonition," Carlotta said to me. "You would have been a Java Green. The original peafowl. Feisty, but not hardy. Their crests don't fan out, but go straight up. They know their importance, the Adams and Eves, but they're modest about it."

"How can you tell?" I asked.

"I can't really. It's only a game I like to play."

"What am I?" Jonis asked.

"I don't know yet."

"Lizzy, will you have me sing something?" Carlotta asked. She asked with such confidence that I feared she may have come prepared with a show tune or two.

"You don't have to sing," I said and deliberated as to whether or not I should explain that if she sang something she would simply be copying the pitches as they've been written for the song and it wouldn't give me much insight into her vocal patterns anyway. I decided against it. "I've just been paying attention to your speaking voice," I said.

"And? Any premonitions of your own?"

"It'll take some thinking on my part," I said. "I've been paying attention to the intervals in which your voice changes, for what reasons you change your pitches. I'll do some studying up with peacock sounds. I suppose I could look up a bit about their vocal cord composition too. I'll certainly let you know what I find."

"I have recordings," she said. "Peacock recordings, if you want them."

"That would be helpful, and it would be nice to actually observe some. Do you have peacocks? I mean do you raise any?"

"No," Carlotta said, hesitantly. "I'm grappling with that. I'd love to have their companionship. I can't think of anything I'd love more. But it doesn't feel right. It's hard to explain, even to myself, but it has to do with superiority. I'd be their caretaker, feeding them, cleaning them. They'd be my animals. I'd be keeping them captive when they should rightly be out in the wild. I would be good to them; you could be sure of that. But nothing being cared for is really free, not a child, or a lover, or a pet."

There was a rustling in the evergreen above us and the sound of cracking bones. The three of us looked up together. A scavenger was picking at the insides of a seagull. He was slow and diligent, perched on a nearby branch and leaning down. He plucked at the feathers – white and grey pieces fell to the ground – then he peeled the meat from the bones. We could hear it, that sultry separation of skin from muscle, muscle from bone. The bird was on his back, head and wings drooped and intertwined in the tree. I gasped and turned my head away.

"Better to be used than to rot away," Carlotta said. A feather fell down into her lap. She picked it up and ran it across her hand. She waited for me to agree or disagree. I looked at Jonis but he seemed also to be waiting. I didn't know what I was to say or do, who I was to either of these strangers sitting before me. They wanted something from me, but what? Devotion? Belief? Evidence against their own suspected artifice? I felt I had let both of them down.

CHAPTER TEN

Dinner One:

Set to the west in Elmira, New York, in a small but modern farmhouse that the Ivanovas had purchased in the late 1970s. Carl and I sat at a wooden dining room table, exchanging worried glances as I refilled my water cup from a pitcher and took slow sips to stay occupied. The men, Inka's father and her younger brother Pad (short for Paddington), and the guests, Carl and I, were seated in what seemed a mandatory silence, while the women of the family clanked dishes, bickered in Russian, and finished up the cooking in the kitchen.

Kimmy, Inka's older sister, came out carrying a glass bowl of lettuce drenched in dressing and placed it on the table. She had recently moved back into her childhood home after a quarrel with her husband, and this baffled Inka who held that even a "good domestic beating would be better than moving back into that house." Kimmy looked like an enlarged version of Inka. She was taller, wider, her facial features more spread out. The extra space was softening; that rounded snout nose, large forehead and breasts that stuck out on Inka's small frame were far less intimidating on Kimmy.

Kimmy pondered the table. There were three vacant chairs, one between Carl and me, one at the head of the table opposite Inka's father, and then a small metal and presumably "guest" chair next to Pad.

"Oh, I can move into that chair," I said and stood.

"Don't be silly. Sit. Have some salad," Kimmy replied. I tried to argue but she pressed on my shoulder decisively as if she would not let me rise.

Kimmy served the salad and took a seat at the head of the table. Inka entered and urged us to begin eating it: "Mom hates when people are waiting for her." Mrs. Ivanova entered with the casserole a minute later. She placed the hot dish on the table and swiftly pulled the chair out from under Kimmy with a huff of aggressive strength that threw Kimmy haphazardly on the floor, as surprised as the rest of us at what had happened. Mrs. Ivanova laughed a quick high giggle, and whacked her oldest daughter over the head with a pot-holder.

It was all like one of those low-budget plays, the ones where the stage is so small and the crew so lacking that there is only one "set" and a seemingly never-ending scene that carries the characters from start to finish. It felt prepared in advance – Pad's silence, Mrs. Ivanova's audacity, Kimmy's recklessness – the script written by Inka to corroborate her position as the sole sane member of a horrid family, a girl to be pitied for her origins and admired for escaping them.

Kimmy pulled up her too-tight jeans and pushed herself to a stand. "There's company, Mom. You're smaller." Kimmy spoke in calm English. Unlike Inka, she had perfectly enunciated words with no trace of an accent.

Mrs. Ivanova looked around for someone else to step in, like she didn't want to be the bad guy for once, but no one said a word. Mrs. Ivanova spoke in Russian: "It's my seat, you idiot," or likely something more derogatory.

Kimmy moved reluctantly to the mismatched metal

chair next to Pad, in which she barley fit, and Mrs. Ivanova began serving generous portions of the casserole. I don't know why Mrs. Ivanova was so taken with the dish, but it was served every time she had company, which mostly meant every time that I came over. The family invited very few people to dinner, and in fact, Inka had never taken home a boy before. Not ever. Carl sat at the table and politely scooped glops of cheesy green beans, carrots, and potatoes into his mouth. I followed suit. No one else seemed to be eating.

"Carl is fluent in Russian," Inka announced to the table. "Also French, and he's pre-med."

Carl's cheeks began to color. I hadn't seen this happen before. Carl was forthcoming and strong. He had approached Inka at the bar on our second visit and asked if she would like to go home with him that night after the bar closed and "get to know each other." It was sweet to see Inka bragging about him.

"What's a person need too many languages for?" Mrs. Ivanova asked in her slightly incorrect English. Her voice rose when she spoke, sharper and sharper, an intergalactic woodpecker. It was maybe the longest phrase I'd ever heard her speak entirely in English.

"You're right," Carl said meekly. "They don't really come in handy all that often."

"You wouldn't get it, Mom," Kimmy said. "Some people like to better themselves." Kimmy paused and chuckled to herself. "That reminds me of this story. When Inka was in fourth grade she stole a pink thong from my bedroom and bartered it to a boy in her class so that he would give her a French kiss, which she had decided must be totally different than a Russian kiss or an English kiss, and she was just dying to find out what the difference was!"

"Kimmy!" Mr. Ivanova barked. "Inappropriate." He was always looking out for his Inka, his youngest. "No one wants to hear that." He paused and looked at his wife.

"And no one wants to eat this. The casserole is watery and tastes like salt."

Mrs. Ivanova threw her fork to the middle of the table and stormed into the kitchen. Kimmy laughed as her mother waddled away and quickly reclaimed the larger chair to finish her dinner.

"You watch it," Mr. Ivanova said to Kimmy.

"Psh, she won't be back," Kimmy replied. "She'll take at least forty-five minutes of huffing and puffing."

Pad, silent and still until this point, began to eat his dinner. "Not bad, actually," he said with his mouth full. He shoveled two more fork-fulls in and then mid-chew let out a sneeze that sent a bean out of his mouth and across the table onto Inka's forearm.

Pad, gangly like Inka and reminiscent of his recently finished teenage gawk, covered his mouth with both hands and laughed with his head back while Inka began a rumbling angry shriek: "You are all disgusting!"

Inka ran to the bathroom and I followed after her.

"It's unbearably awful to be a part of this family," Inka said to me through a crack in the door. I pushed it open and leaned my back gently on the warm radiator. "Is Carl still out there with them?" she asked.

"Unless he stood up and made a run for it."

"Don't you dare joke with me right now."

"Yes, he's out there. Of course he is. You know that."

"Why are you in here then, Lizzy? You were supposed to be the buffer! You were supposed to make him feel like he wasn't the only outsider!"

Inka was sitting on the toilet with her pants pulled down as a matter of habit, but she wasn't going to the bathroom.

"I'll go," I said and turned for the door.

"No, wait," Inka vacillated. "Oh, God! He'll never come back here. It's basically over."

"Stop freaking out and pull up your pants," I said. She did, though reluctantly. "I'm sure he'll understand.

Practically no one has a sane family these days." I considered telling Inka about my parents' separate bedrooms but I knew she would deem it inconsequential in comparison with her troubles. "It'll be fine, Inka, you'll see. We better both get back to Carl before your father starts in on pre-marital sex."

"Oh God! Oh God! Oh God!" Inka chanted.

When we returned to the table Carl had regained the air of cool that had won Inka over in the first place. He was telling one of his "true story … a guy walks into a bar" jokes, based on his real-life experiences, and the Ivanovas (all but Mrs., who had not yet returned) were laughing comfortably with their mouths full and their elbows on the table. Inka sat down with an expression pure and uninhibited, an expression of relief and gratitude. She was for the briefest moment not playing a role, not worrying about how she appeared to others or judging the way that others appeared to her. Inka's script had run out and the play had ended differently than expected. Inka looked at Carl with something like love and in that moment she was beautiful.

Dinner Two:

My mom had lost her kitchen scissors and this was apparently a big deal. She needed them to prepare the chicken we were having that night. She blamed me first, for hiding them, but by the time I started explaining that I didn't even live there, so how could I have hidden them, she was on to accusing my father.

"Did you even check the garage?" she asked. "You can't keep taking my things out there just for whatever reason."

"I didn't take the scissors," my father said.

"First the masking tape, now the kitchen scissors."

"I didn't take the damn masking tape."

Dad shrugged at me and applied some chapstick.

"Would you go and check my bedroom?" my mother asked me, and though I doubted that the scissors were in the bedroom, I was, sadly, as glad to get out of that room as I had been to escape unscathed from the Ivanovas' dinner two nights prior.

Our hallway had gray and white carpet that extended from the bathroom down to what used to be my parents' bedroom. Growing up in a house with all gray carpet and all white walls, I always longed for color. Childhood drawings of my future homes were full of yellows and oranges. The first thing Inka and I did when we moved into our apartment was to paint the walls a different color in each room. If my parents had been more playful with design, maybe they would have been happier.

The hallway felt dull, as usual, but it also held an eerie emptiness. I walked up and down it searching for the difference and found a series of telling nail holes where pictures had been removed. I closed my eyes to see them. One – a wedding photo snapped before my parents' lips touched for a kiss. My mother adorned in white, her neck long and pale, her hair tied in a bun. Two – a picture from the lake. My mother sat in the sand and my father stood sporting an old-fashioned suit, short shorts up his thighs in neon red. Three – a hole on the wall. I couldn't remember it. I touched the vacant spot with my palm.

The last time I had visited, the master bedroom belonged only to my mother. Now, piles of my father's blue sweaters rose up from the floor, the bed was unmade and Dad's telltale empty water bottles lined the nightstand. For a moment I was hopeful that my father had moved back in, that the trouble was over, then I glanced across the hall to the open door of *my* old bedroom where my mother's bottles of perfume, hairspray, and body lotion sat out on my dresser. I imagined some sort of negotiation where my father expressed his love and in exchange for this love was given rights to the master bedroom, or maybe they had arm-wrestled for it, or flipped a coin.

"Did you find them?" my mother called from the kitchen.

I didn't even know which room I was supposed to be looking in. I scanned one and then the other. I saw no scissors and I didn't care to look harder. I sprayed my mother's Black Pearls perfume into the air. At least *it* was the same. I closed my eyes and sat on my childhood bed. From that scent I could feel her there in the room with me, tucking me in with her soft night words, that whir of *G flat* in the darkness.

The chicken turned out well, despite the missing scissors, though I did wonder what had happened to them. Had my father hidden them in a passive-aggressive rage? Had my mother misplaced them and just couldn't help but spread the blame elsewhere? My parents seemed so petty and small, and I hated not admiring them.

After dinner my father sat in the living room in his beige corduroy recliner, a piece of furniture my mother openly despised. It was not dirty or torn, it roughly match-ed our forest green couches, but it smelled, my mother insisted, like an old lady. It had come from a garage sale and my father adored it. He sat there, feet up and crossed at the ankles, crossword in lap. He cracked open peanut shells and placed them in his mouth to devour in a quick crunch. My mother was sprawled on the couch, pillow under neck; she instinctively winced each time the sound of the peanut crack echoed. I wondered if there wasn't one thing she still loved about him.

What had been the point of my parents' lives togeth-er? I *was* vain enough to think that I had been the point, but there in our living room it didn't seem enough. I was greedy for the ending I had expected, for my own children in that living room, crawling rampantly over the matted gray rug. I wanted a mirror, an inversion, the world open-ing out (college, love, a profession) and then pulling back in again (marriage, children, a family with grandparents and happy stories of childhood). I wanted a closed universe, not an ever-expanding world where eventually things moved so far apart that nothing could be as it once was, life torn particle by particle: limb from body, skin from bone, protons from neutrons, quarks from gluons, never to assemble again.

"Play something for us, Lizzy," my mother requested. It was the only part of the evening that felt at all usual.

Out of spite I didn't want to perform any act that would bring either of them joy; but more, I didn't want to sit and listen to their silent argument of peanut cracks and cringes.

I played Pachelbel's Canon in D, starting in the middle where the cannon is denser and the notes quicker. I couldn't take the tantalizing emotion of the opening. The sound of the piano resonated differently that night. It did not rise or ring. It was dull like the ceiling had been brought down or the walls carpeted, though of course they had not been. The problem was us, my mother, my father and me – we all seemed to take up more space. We were wide and dense with our own bottled sorrows and we dampened the sound.

Dinner Three:

The windows in the Starks' house exposed the living room and kitchen to the country road outside. Usually the curtains were kept closed but tonight they'd been tied aside and we sat at the table and watched the sky fading to dark, the trees turning to fall. It was one of those nights when the trees come alive along the side of the road. All shapes and sizes and different shades of yellow-orange, not yet red; it wasn't late enough in the season for red. The leaves, like palms of an articulate hand, turned upward and then down again. When I was young my dad told me that when the leaves turned upside-down they were signaling rain and I remember my awe. I hadn't known that the trees had a language. With this knowledge the world changed for me: the grass whispered in the night outside my bedroom window, the trees threw their heads back in laughter or fury, the flowers bent toward the sun and sighed like sunbathers as they soaked it in. As I sat beside Jonis, now, the earth around me was acutely alive, speaking in its windswept howls and silently singing leaves; it had been a while since I'd heard it.

There was a commotion in the living room that opened up through a rounded archway behind us. Patty had her hands full of strange objects and threw them all down onto the sofa: a pair of socks, two flattened pennies from highway rest-stop tourist sights, a tarnished ring, a wooden whistle. Patty came into the kitchen and began washing out a round-bottomed fishbowl.

"There hasn't been a fish in here since Jonis was little," she said to me. "But it's come to other uses."

"Lando," Jonis said. "He lived for six years."

"We buried him in a sewer. Where was it?" Patty asked.

"Hoboken. I played the recorder. I was big on the recorder then."

"Treacherous instrument!" Patty laughed from her eyes and her cheeks. I hadn't seen her laugh this way before.

Jonis picked up his crutches and went over to the refrigerator for some cold cuts. He pulled a fresh loaf of Italian bread off the counter, tomatoes from a bowl. The table was really only big enough for two, and when Patty finished cleaning the fishbowl and came to sit beside us, my elbow bumped her as I reached for my dinner. She caught my arm and pretended to karate chop it off.

"People should gather in the evening and practice kung-fu together instead of sitting around and eating, don't you think? That would make for a healthier, stronger America."

"If only you'd been around for the initiation of family

values, Mom, things would be much less dull."

I took a bite of my sandwich. Though there was nowhere else I wanted to be, this certainly didn't feel like home. I missed the slow process of childhood dinners: My mother peeking in from her post in the kitchen to see what my father and I were laughing at on the TV. The layering of odors, first pure – garlic and butter in the pan – and then a steady build of content that let us guess which meal was being prepared. A shrimp and asparagus pasta. A lemon butter chicken. My most recent meal at home had proved that all of that was over.

"I wonder what it would have been like to have a daughter," Patty said. "Maybe I'll have one yet."

"You mean a daughter-in-law," Jonis said knocking me on the arm.

"No, I meant a real one."

Jonis rolled his eyes.

"I'm kidding," Patty said. "Lizzy knew I was kidding."

I nodded. I was always nodding at her.

I wondered what my mother would think of Patty. She might call her hard or she might call her strong. Patty had no attachments to anyone or anything but her son. She had lived in different houses, in different towns and cities all across New York, New Jersey, Connecticut, any place that was close enough to make monthly visits to the NYC hospitals. Before Jonis, she had traveled extensively: Italy, China, Peru, Jordan. She was no one's subordinate, she had never been married, and had been working for herself since she was twenty-two. Patty was so many of the things that my mother was not. I imagined my mother trying to latch onto her and absorb her, an embarrassing thought; I didn't want them to meet.

"For all my studies of gender issues and women's rights, I don't know if I would have been good at it," Patty said. "I might have been too hard on a daughter. If you get in a girl's way it alters her path. She ends up choosing to spite those around her instead of finding out what she truly has affinities for."

"You? Not good at something?" Jonis said.

Patty shrugged and rose. She put the objects from the couch into the fishbowl and then went into her bedroom and came out with a new pile in her arms: the empty packaging of a chocolate bar and a notebook with a log cabin on the cover. She stuffed in a black t-shirt, a dried leaf, a miniature black stapler. She placed the fishbowl on the mantle above the fireplace and took a seat on the couch to read a book on the sacred landscapes of India. She and Jonis were both reading it and they had a tentative trip planned for the following year.

"What's with the fishbowl?" I whispered, and Jonis mouthed: "Explain later."

He put his hand on mine under the table. I saw there was a little bit of mayonnaise on the top of his index finger that he wiped off onto my jeans; he didn't know I noticed.

In Jonis's room we sat against the mahogany back-board on a bed that extended across the room from one wall to the other. On the TV mounted on the wall, we watched a show about a ridiculously broken family, or wasn't that all shows, and all families? Jonis was the only one that I told about my parents' separation, or whatever it was. My father had called me that afternoon to let me know that my mother had taken off her ring. I wanted Inka to know. I even wanted Joe to know. I practiced telling them at night. They would hug me and brush my hair with their hands. They would understand my loss in a way others couldn't, because they knew my parents well, my father's fragility, my mother's honesty. They had been doted on and loved by both of my parents, especially my mother.

My mother had always been upfront about her life and expected that people would be upfront about theirs as well; with her they usually were. She knew all about Inka's difficult childhood and about Joe's rejection by his older brothers who thought that a career in music was "frivolous" and "gay." And they knew about her, her bouts of depression during pregnancy, her hatred for her boss at work (before she retired), her fantasy of being a hostess on a cruise ship. They knew how close she had always been to me but they didn't know that all of her "openness" had ended. Three months had passed in which she did not speak to me of her mid-life crisis, and I did not speak to her of mine or of my father's sadness.

Inka and Joe could have mourned this loss of friendship and openness in a way that Jonis could not, but Joe and I hardly talked once a week, avoiding our deteriorating relationship, and Inka hadn't been doing much listening lately. There was no one to tell but Jonis, and when I did he hugged me but did not tell me that things would work themselves out. He said "ouch" like a Band-Aid pulled off quickly and that was all he said.

The episode ended.

"Another?" Jonis asked. He had the chutzpah to stay up all night, any night, even though he awoke for work much earlier than I did.

"I'm tired," I said and made a cockeyed sad face.

"I wonder how I could convince you never to make that face again," Jonis said, leaning his face into mine.

Jonis sat up and began to unravel the stern white compression bandages from around his leg. They were splotched with the usual blood. Lofts of bandages filled his closets, for he rewrapped each morning and night, applied his medications, and allowed his leg to breath for a while before he wrapped it up again. It was a careful process, not to scratch or irritate, not to wrap so tight as to cut off circulation, but tight enough to pressure the pain of thick varicose veins into submission.

"There was a nurse named Miranda," Jonis told me as he unraveled. "She taught me how tight to pull and how much blood was enough for alarm. She was my first love."

"How old were you?"

"Eleven, when I first met her. She was on night shifts so she'd be there late when it was quiet and early when the sun came up and glared in through the hospital windows. She would say, 'You must wake your leg up slowly.' She would stretch it out along the white hospital sheets and nod her head in approval. One morning I asked her how much longer she thought it would grow, and she said, 'As long as you can handle, I suppose.' I've repeated that phrase so many times to myself: as long as I can handle."

I reached for Jonis's medication on his nightstand and began to apply it to the parts of his leg that he could not easily reach on his own. It was a cake-beige cream with a noxious odor.

"Miranda was the only nurse who worked my leg with bare hands. You remind me of her," Jonis said.

"Of your adolescent crush? I don't know how to feel about that."

"Not like that. She was young, beautiful, too beautiful to care about me, but she really saw me, you know? I can't explain it. She didn't look past my leg or at it; she just saw, like you do. She was gentle with her seeing."

As I massaged in his medicine it was gentle that I tried for and wanted. There was a turn in my stomach as I touched his scarred, discolored skin, moist and acrid from the day but I would not allow myself to cringe or retreat. I helped Jonis to rewrap his leg for the night, taking tips on where to overlap, where to tighten, and then I went to the bathroom and scrubbed my hands for the time it took for me to sing "Twinkle, Twinkle, Little Star," as I had been taught by my father.

When I returned to the bedroom the rain had begun, pulsing, beating with more sounds than I could account for though my mind sped off trying. It was meaningless to attempt to decode the music of rain: it was not music at all; it had no organization or refrain. I had told myself all of this before but still I tried to find it, a hidden logic, a composition that only I could hear.

"All that stuff my mom had in the fishbowl," Jonis said, "they're memories: things from her old boyfriends, travels, days or moments she considers important."

He instructed me to reach underneath his bed and pull out a box that was housed there, a wooden box with an octopus chiseled imperfectly on the front. I handed it over to him.

"Is there anything in the fishbowl from your father?" I asked.

"Something in there must be, but she'd never tell me what."

"You never met him?"

"If I did, I can't remember. I can't remember any men, but when I was younger I'd find things in her bedroom, letters, photos…"

"A snooper?"

"I was, but it didn't turn out to be an effective method of getting to know anything. I'm not anymore."

"She doesn't really seem the nostalgic type," I said.

"Oh, she is. She believes in constructive nostalgia." He opened his box. "She gave me this box to start collecting my memories when I was in the fourth grade. She said that collecting important pieces of your past helps you to believe that what happened really happened, and can't be changed. She thinks that collecting memories and mementoes keeps the past where it should be, in a box, or a fishbowl, so you don't have to spend your time questioning, recollecting, and reminiscing. Once in a while she takes things out, looks them over, and reminds herself how she got to be where she is."

He unfolded a piece of paper entitled: *Why?* "Doug and I used to come up with them after school when we were in fourth grade. Sometimes my mom helped."

Jonis pointed out some of his favorites.

4. I am an alien from Pluto sent down to warn the human race of an infectious virus that will be striking them soon.

21. I got caught in a taffy pull when I was seven and the doctors haven't been able to figure out how to fix it yet, though one of them almost tried taking a bite to see what flavor I was.

38. God lost his ruler when I was created and despite what you might think he's not very good at math.

46. Two words: mall escalator.

"I was in a wheelchair that year. The leg was too heavy for me. It was the year they started discussing amputation."

"And why didn't you … why haven't you?"

Jonis closed his box like a mouth chomping down. "Why haven't you cut off your leg?" he asked. It was too harsh, instinctual, he closed his eyes as if to reset and then opened the octopus box again and pulled out a Polaroid of himself dated 1987. In the photo he is four. He is standing on top of a hill wearing a blue sweater, acid-washed jeans, and sneakers.

"Look at what I was," Jonis said. I touched the glossy child with my fingers; he looked out at me and I recognized that boy as if I'd always known him.

"Do you really feel you were different then?" I asked. "I think I've always been the same. As far back as I can remember what it was like to be inside my head, I recall thinking the same way, feeling things in the same way."

"I don't know if I was different, per se, but when I think back to who I was then I can sense a quality that I've lost. I miss him, or me, that version of me," Jonis said.

I allowed the image in the photograph to animate with wind, sound, and movement…

"Watch me," young Jonis says as he drops to the ground. His lanky arms extend above his head and he begins another tumble down the sloping mound, accelerating against the air as if nothing could ever stop him. The bristles of grass prickle Jonis's young skin like medical needles on that sunny day in the suburbs.

Patty looks up from her book. It's brightly colored and from the medical section of the local used bookstore. She has already begun her urgent search to know more than the doctors. The sound of laughter is coming from the other children who roll alongside Jonis. They run from swing set to slide to see-saw to the hill and Jonis reaches the bottom just in time to land atop a friend, laughing. It is the last warm day of fall and the children run like they know this. There's an excitement before a cold winter that coats children with energy. Imagining a chilling hibernation, the coolness of October is freeing; beneath jackets and sweatshirts the body grows sticky so that it's possible to stay comfortably outside until the moms call them in for dinner.

After rolling once, Jonis and his friends run back up the hill together, Jonis in the lead despite his slightly swollen and irregular right foot.

"We need a bigger hill," Jonis calls out, looking around to see if there is one. "Bigger and faster!"

Jonis's jeans have dinosaurs on the back pockets. His two high-top sneakers light up when he steps. I can see him as clearly as if he were my own child, alive, real, standing before me in that bedroom where I lay. Waiting to take my hand, to run and jump and begin the day. I want to have met him, to have held him. The children follow Jonis's lead to a larger hill behind them. They climb it and roll. Climb and roll as fast as possible, running out of time.

"I'd like you to meet my doctor," Jonis said. The water was pounding on the four-paned window behind, an anxious intruder. "He's been with me from the start. He's the only male role model I've had in my life."

I felt relieved by the request, like meeting this man would somehow connect me to the boy in the photograph, the child that Patty kept her memories of in a fishbowl, and that Jonis still longed for.

As I drove home from Jonis and Patty's house that night the windshield wipers squeaked as they flicked the rain. Ithaca was wet and messy with puddles of leaves and drooping naked trees. I had thought of getting new wipers put on the last time that it rained, and now I thought of it again.

I had gotten my two-door Honda Civic new from a dealership. My father and I picked it out. "It's a good car," he told me. "Small enough to fit in a tight parking spot, but still safe." In reality *he* picked out the car but I was there to concur. I told him I loved it. I got to choose between white and black and black seemed more triumphant. That day I drove it home, the cloth seats seemed cleaner than anything I'd touched before. It had that new-car smell, which ironically reminded me of old library books, and everything worked. I never worried about the transmission, the brakes, or the fact that all I'd actually contributed with my own funds was a steering wheel cover. It felt as much mine as if I had bought it, since true ownership of anyone or anything was then still a foreign concept to me. I didn't realize until later that it was possible I might never own a new car again. I might never be able to afford on my own what my father so willingly gave me. It might have been better to have grown up like my parents did, with nothing. I know that this is a privileged thought. My parents worked very hard and their worlds expanded outwards. It felt like mine would only ever implode.

The squeak was irritating, pitched A to C, and irregular in its volume, much louder on some swipes than on others. I didn't want to hear it anymore. I didn't want to be out driving in the dark rain, or to do the three tunings I had scheduled for the next morning. I only wanted to be beside Jonis, listening to his small confessions, imagining the life he had lived before he knew me, and the one we'd someday live together.

My cellphone rang and surprised me. I pulled the wheel too hard to the right and hydroplaned. *Don't brake. Don't brake.* I let the water control me until I could steer out of it. Joe's name was on the screen. His greeting sounded awkward, stifled. I asked him where he was. I pictured him in the bathroom at a strange woman's apartment, crouched on the toilet and cupping his hand over the mouthpiece of the phone to muffle the sound of his speaking. Nothing about the woman still sleeping in her bed outside that bathroom door seemed disconcerting. It was as if she'd always been there.

"I'm at home," he said. "Where are you?"

"I'm driving. It's awful here, cold and rainy. Why haven't we taken off to a warmer climate yet?"

"I don't know," Joe said. "Why haven't we?"

The wipers were increasing in volume and I listened to them rather than to the silence on the line.

"Hello?" I asked, after a while.

"Hello," Joe answered back.

It had been three weeks since I'd last called Joe and left him one of my daily messages. During that time he had sung to me twice, in the middle of the night, sad songs.

"Were you ever going to call again?" He cleared his throat – a cough, a sob? "Forget it," he said. "I'm calling because something came up and I thought of you."

"How *nice* of you, Joey."

"You only call me that when you're angry. No one else calls me that."

"Another syllable, that's all."

Sqeeeek. Squeeeek. *A* to *C. A* to *C.*

"The Opera has been organizing a group to tour city high schools and community centers, to raise interest for the arts and theater within the boroughs. All the shows are free admission, and the performers are all volunteering our time. The Opera's letting us use costumes and props and rehearsal space so the show is pretty good. Our pianist backed out and we haven't had a new volunteer come forward. I told them I knew someone."

"Oh."

"It's a mish-mash of stuff," he said. I imagined this was one of his new phrases. Something he'd picked up from a new friend. He was always picking up little tics from others and then exploiting them. I bet he cooked up mish-mash dinners from whatever was left in his fridge and threw on a mish-mash of whichever of his clothes weren't dirty. "The performance is called *Looking Forward: Greats of the Twentieth Century*. Messiaen, Debussy, Foss, Stravinsky … you'd like it."

"Oh."

"Stop saying oh, Lizzy, and tell me what you think. It's seven performances over two weeks You're one of the only people I know that'd be able to learn the music fast enough but you'll have to come down ASAP to rehearse with us."

I had for so long expected that this would happen, that Joe would pull me into his world. "I don't know," I said. "I have a lot going on here."

"Really?" Joe said. "Like what?"

"I don't know, piano tuning, plans with friends, my life."

"And a fucking handicapped boyfriend?"

"What?"

"Inka told me."

The conversation must have started so innocently. "Joe, it's been so long. How *are* you? Tell me everything." Inka would make him believe that she missed him innocently and then she'd turn it: "Speaking of Lizzy, there's something I've been meaning to tell you…" It was not an unexpected betrayal but I felt so childish, sitting there in my car wishing I could strangle Inka, wishing I had told him first.

"You left me," I said. I wondered if he could hear the wipers squawking. I wondered if I sounded like them.

Joe inhaled slow and audibly, as if preparing to sing. "Let me know by the end of the week if you'll come."

The line went silent. I missed the sound of the dial tone, a constant companion that would stay with you as long as you cared to keep the phone to your ear, or almost. As a child I would listen to see if the pitch of the "beep-beep-beep" would change. I always hoped that it might turn into a song, that if I listened long enough I'd be rewarded with a secret track. But instead, there would arise the sharp voice of a woman, urging me to return the phone to its base. The "beep" was slightly higher or lower on different phones and during different months, but once it started up at the end of a call it never did give way to a more interesting melody. And that woman, I pictured her young and pretty; she was probably long dead by the time I heard her but she always sounded the same.

CHAPTER ELEVEN

Jonis, Patty, and I approached the Children's Hospital of New York, a strong brick building, uninviting from the street with its new construction and blocky exterior; but inside, I'd find it was a bright warm place full of noise and motion. Jonis pulled into a handicapped parking space outside the hospital's main entrance on 168th Street. In Jonis's car there was no center panel with a radio, there was no armrest, or strange pointless hump between the seats. There was instead a long soft area extending down into a cavern, a large doggy bed with fluffy white fabric where Jonis's leg could comfortably reside. Dr. Kershner had helped Jonis to design it, something accommodating and comfortable. It made all other cars seem predictable.

"For a short rebellious period in his late teens, Jonis refused the convenience of handicapped parking, not wanting to allow himself anything that a 'normal' person wouldn't have," Patty explained to me. "During his early twenties he had flipped the game and abused the privilege, handing out handicapped stickers to all his friends from college."

Jonis rolled his eyes at his mother's over-sharing.

"And now?" I asked.

She gesticulated her hand out the window towards the demanding Handicapped Parking sign before us, its bold un-inclusive blue that drew closer as we pulled in.

"Stop talking about me like I'm not here," Jonis said, adding nothing about his opinion on the matter. He pressed down the parking break with his left foot and slid the key out of its slot with care. Jonis meticulously ordered his movements, prearranged and paced in a well choreographed dance. It appeared that the conveniently located handicapped spots had come to feel appropriate to Jonis, even respectable. He accepted his spot and the short walk it offered us on that hot gray afternoon in Washington Heights.

Walking into the hospital seemed for Jonis somewhat like what returning to my old elementary school was for me. I visited frequently since my father was still working there. Things were too small, too bright, and only vaguely recognizable. Everything spurred on a slightly inaccurate memory, a boy named Steve who used to kiss my hand, a milk carton I spilled and left unaccounted for, as I shamefully ran back to my classroom. My father's co-workers, who had also been my teachers, remembered little things about my seven- or eight- or nine-year-old self. My first-grade teacher, Mrs. Pine, recalled that I was afraid to push hard on the chalk foreseeing that it might break, so my letters and numbers were faint and unreadable when it was my turn at the board. Mrs. Ostrie (kindergarten) spoke of a particular girl who stole my food at snack time and recalled how she urged me to defend myself, never successfully. To these memories that were not my own, I had no way to connect.

In a similar way, as Jonis passed through colorful halls of the hospital, he caught sight of things attached to him. He pointed out the spot where the old popcorn maker used to be, his favorite view of the courtyard where he spend many a day gazing out, the room, 205, where his friend Lenny had died. I followed behind Jonis and Patty as we walked towards the most prominent attachment, and the reason that I had come along.

Dr. Kershner sat in his office and picked at the edge of his desk, which was a gaping wooden wound. Patty charged through the door and held it open for Jonis and me behind her. She sat upon one of the worn-out chairs opposite the doctor's desk. Dr. Kershner probably had other patients who knocked on the door politely before they entered, or who waited for an invitation to be seated.

"You'll ruin the desk that way," Patty said.

Dr. Kershner stopped his picking and placed his hands in his lap. He was a wormy man, slender, bald, and as white as his coat.

"What's up, Doc?" Jonis said without a smile. I imagined this was a longstanding tradition that had begun when he was a gangly boy and Bugs Bunny was still somewhat popular.

"Hi, Jonis," the doctor said, nodding.

I was hanging in the doorway admiring the walls of the office that were filled almost entirely with pictures from children. Centered above the doctor's desk there was a colorful compilation of sea creatures signed at the bottom with Jonis's distinctive looping "J."

Jonis looked back for me. "I brought someone to meet you, Doc," he said. I stepped forward and the doctor shook my hand with a convincing grip.

"I've heard you're a musician," Dr. Kershner said. I blushed to think of them discussing me. "My daughter's in the theater program at Sarah Lawrence. She went back last month for her junior year."

"Good old Sarah Lawrence," Patty said with a smug smile, reminding the doctor that she had gone there as well.

"She sings," Dr. Kershner added.

"She must love it," I said, because though I hadn't most people who are performance majors do.

"She'll never be as happy as she is right now, I keep

on telling her," he said.

"What an awful thing to say," Patty said and I agreed. It might be the worst thing that anyone could ever tell you.

"You tell her I said hi." Jonis said. He turned his gaze to me. "Amy and I had a game we played in the hospital one summer where we pretended we were constantly making our escape from a mysterious villain in black. Anyone in the hospital wearing black could serve as the culprit. We'd creep through the halls, hiding in vacant rooms and closets, and one day we popped out and scared a nurse so badly she freaked out."

"I wouldn't say she freaked out," the doctor said. "She fell and hit her head on a counter and got a concussion. And I had to get a sitter for the remainder of the summer to keep Amy out of here and out of trouble."

"It was a fun summer," Jonis said. Jonis pulled his car keys out of his back pocket and hung them on a screw of his crutch.

"Why do you let him drive all this way?" the doctor asked of Patty.

"What do you think we went to all the trouble of his car for?"

"It's best for the leg to be elevated during extended periods of sitting," Dr. Kershner said.

"He's fine, *Doctor.*"

That she still allowed him his title must have surprised him. She spoke to him like an ex-husband to whom she had been married briefly and estranged for years and maybe she had been.

"There's a new, more porous wrapping material that they're trying out," the doctor said, getting down to business. "It's supposed to increase circulation while still holding the skin tight enough to ease the pain and constrict the varicose veins. I've heard good things about it," he said.

Dr. Kershner handed Jonis a folder of papers which included information on this new wrapping fabric and a number of other new findings which had arisen in the past months in respect to tumorous growths, varicose veins, extreme swelling, circulation issues, and any of the eight genetic diseases which Jonis was classified as being related to. The papers were stapled together carefully, arranged from most to least interesting, just as they had been for the past five years since Jonis first requested these updates. Jonis leafed through them quickly before they moved on from the office to a colorful children's check-up station down the hall.

In the small exam room I stood against the wall and Patty sat in a chair in the corner clutching her purse, tightly, a strength exercise. Patty thought it important for a woman to be physically strong. She kept in good shape with the practicing of different martial arts. She called herself a "martial arts slut": karate, krav maga, kung fu, tae kwon do, tai chi, gatka, aikido. There were so many to try, developed by different cultures and times. She stuck with some long enough for introduction, and others for subtle mastery, but could never choose one to settle on for good.

Patty's eyes perused the alphabet-letter wallpaper: *Z is for zebra*, and *L is for lion*. She seemed sad, helpless, almost childlike herself. Perhaps she was thinking of the way it had been different when Jonis was a boy. Of the silliness that parents can conjure so easily when their children are young. Perhaps she thought of how useful she had been then, how necessary. When Jonis was a boy she must have stood beside him, held his hand. I wondered if she could recall exactly when she stopped, that moment when Jonis was too old, when she first sat back in the provided chair, waited, crossed and uncrossed her legs.

Dr. Kershner snapped on the sterile gloves and unwrapped Jonis's bandages. He began at the knee and looped away the gauze with his flicking wrist until all of Jonis's leg was revealed. It did not fit on the child-sized examining table, even with an extension placed at the end, a cold metal surface.

"I'm really beginning to outgrow this room," Jonis said with a laugh.

"You never fit to begin with," the doctor replied. Though in truth he once had, an infant, a child, a boy prophesied to deformity and carefully watched as he came into it.

Dr. Kershner touched the leg gently as you would a scraped knee. Every time I saw his leg exposed I examined it anew. It was so pale compared to the rest of him, untouched by the sun of the hot New York summer just past. Today the leg had a patchy red texture, dots and lines the color of tongue, some blood escaped the skin and some lay beneath. By the end of the exam the doctor was squatting on the floor, looking over the foot, the toes, the heel, the swollen, fleshy disfigurement. He felt for new lumps and asked, "Have you any sensation when I touch here? How about here?" He stood up from the floor and focused on the top of the leg once again.

"The tumor below the knee seems to be holding, but you need to keep a close eye on it. Any increase in size at all and we should remove it. The skin on the foot is infected, but not worse than it has been," Dr. Kershner said. "Have you given any more thought to amputation?"

A clot at the door stopped the air and killed everything inside; the room went still. This had all happened before, and it would happen again. I was the only variable and I knew what I must do.

"What are the risks and benefits?" I asked boldly. To my surprise, when my sound hit the room no pose or expression changed but my own. I thought they might ignore me and I felt a fury building. Then, Patty turned to face me with the same seething expression she had been focusing on Dr. Kershner, and I only wished that I had been ignored.

"The amputation involves risks, of course," Dr. Kershner said to me. "There is, of course, the risk of the surgery itself. Then, there could be infection. There is a relatively high chance that the limb could keep growing after the amputation, that tumors would continue to need removal on the affected limb. Keeping the situation as it is has its own risks of infection, as well as that of blood clots and heart attacks, which an amputation would drastically reduce. An amputation would make Jonis more mobile; he would be a candidate for a prosthetic, and prosthetics are getting ever more advanced."

"Thank you," I whispered, having lost my gumption. Patty looked away from me and walked out of the room. Jonis and I shook hands with the doctor and slowly followed.

We walked through the boisterous halls and I kept my eyes down, deciding if I should apologize, what for and to whom.

"They used to have these giant paintings of the Sesame Street characters on the walls," Jonis said, "saying hopeful things like *Strength Comes From Within*. Lenny had this habit of sneaking out of his room at night and drawing mustaches on them with a black permanent marker he kept in a hole in the windowsill. Petey was my best friend, and he was the one who figured it out. Petey could tell by the way Lenny smiled when the nurses found his 'artwork' in the morning. Petey told everyone. I mean every kid, no authorities, of course, and Lenny became a sort of hero. No one ever ratted him out. There was no room for bullying, no traitors among the sick."

"How old was he ... Lenny?" I asked.

"Eleven when he died. Cancer. I was nine and I was in for three weeks for tests and a tumor removal. I watched him turn into a skeleton and disappear. It was my first death and so I thought that's how it always happened, the hair and then the color and then the flesh and then life altogether. I had no idea that there were other more sudden ways to die, that you could be fine and normal looking one day and gone the next. I'd find that out later."

I left a moment to picture him, this skeleton boy, wise

and hairless in a way I wasn't yet near to being, sneaking through the hall and defacing the false hope he couldn't possibly believe in.

"I'm sorry," I said.

"Oh, don't even worry. She'll be over it by the time we get into the car."

"No…" I said, but then left it.

He didn't need my sorrow and neither did Lenny, but I was sorry. I was sorry for my own childhood, for that time when I believed that life was fair, not in a "God is just" or even karmic sense, less complicated, more basic. I believed that there was a balance between the good and the bad in people's lives. I would find myself examples of this balance. For instance, Kimberly Kwan of my fourth-grade class got the lead in the school play but her favorite grandfather died later that year. I was rightly acknowledging the mixture between joy and despair that we will all encounter, but I was wrongly justifying that we, all human beings, were dealt an even share of it. This false sense of balance alleviated any jealousy I felt towards others, or any guilt I felt when my life seemed to be going too well. I believed in equality, that people around the world had equal parts happiness and sadness, just like I did. Walking through the halls of the Children's Hospital of New York I felt ashamed that I had ever been able to be so naïve. I went for too long knowing too little about the greater world, its horror, its malice, its terrible lack of integrity. Growing up, Jonis had no such illusions. He had seen for himself a very different kind of world.

CHAPTER TWELVE

We were on our way into the dollar store for cheap balloons. My arm was linked under Jonis's, and his arm over
the side of his crutch; it was a thing we were trying. His
crutch hit my foot and I pulled away, throwing him off
balance. He teetered but did not fall.

"Didn't work out," I said.

"Practice makes perfect?" Jonis asked.

Jonis grabbed my arm and linked it under his once
again. We proceeded more slowly this time and must have
looked silly. An elderly woman with a cane turned her head
as she passed us by. A young couple holding hands whispered sweet nothings at our expense. A man in a truck
slowed and glared at us out his window before proceeding.

There was a boy in the parking lot with a black mop
of hair, a pale angular face and a bulbous nose. His mother
may have been Asian and his father Italian, or the other
way around. He was slender but strong, dribbling a basketball with a group of boys taller and probably older. The
ball hitting the pavement as it passed from boy to boy was
an aggressive sound, moving closer until it was right upon
us. I jumped back as the ball passed beside me, inches
away, and hurried us up near the store, *Everything a Dollar*,

and opened the door for Jonis. As he prepared to walk in, the boy from the lot threw the basketball so that it bounced off of Jonis's crutch and was diverted a ways down the sidewalk.

"Sorry, man," the boy called. "Can you get that for me?" His friends giggled, and turned away but the boy stood facing Jonis, his arms at his sides, shoulders back. Jonis looked at me and smiled.

"Don't…" I said.

Jonis crutched down the walk where the ball continued to roll until it hit against a garbage can, giving Jonis a chance to catch up. He adjusted himself so he could kick the ball back into the parking lot with his good leg by balancing momentarily on his crutches. His kick was good, straight and practiced. The ball landed at the boy's feet. Jonis started back to the door I was holding for him.

"Nice shot, man. You should join the special Olympics or something," the boy called, causing his friends to roar with laughter.

"Shut up!" I called with the intention of heading over there, of, I don't know, throwing his stupid basketball hard against his head. Jonis hung his weight on my arm in protest so that I couldn't get away without causing him to fall. "Apologize!" I screeched and by then I could hear myself, the unpleasant judder of strained vocal chords, of sound moved without breath or space.

The boy's friends laughed ever harder as the culprit himself stood still and smirking. He knew that there was nothing I could do to him, no way to erase what he had said. His mockery had been, like all acts of harm, a way for him to assert his power.

"You're nothing," I said to him. I looked into his eyes. "Nothing." And I could see that he had been told this before.

Jonis finally managed to yank me inside the store where we found ourselves surrounded by aisles of miscellaneous objects: soap dishes, mini kites, hair ties, candy canes, those little umbrellas you put in drinks. Jonis motioned me to the back of the store where we hid behind a shelf of miniature footballs.

"He's a stupid kid. You can't get so worked up," Jonis lectured.

"You could have walked up to him, told him about yourself, made him understand that you're a person, that what he says has consequences."

"I've been this way my whole life. You don't think I know how to handle it?"

The place smelled of mothballs and detergent. Everything was wrapped in plastic. Jonis stood before me, his face red, his hand still on my arm as if I might make an escape.

"How did you handle it?" I asked.

"By walking away. By moving on and not letting it get to me. You need to respect that."

"It's not only you; it's me. He insulted me, too."

Jonis laughed and I pulled my arm away so that we were no longer touching. I didn't think it was funny. I wanted to be able to stand up for him like he would have done for me if some jerk in the parking lot had called out a sexist slur.

"You're an asshole, and that kid's an asshole. The world is full of assholes!" I declared.

I stormed over to the balloon aisle and I heard Jonis following me: click and step, click and step.

"What kind of balloons did Inka want?" Jonis asked.

"Whatever."

The bags of balloons were separated by color, the choices were blue, green, red, or yellow. Jonis grabbed a few bags of each.

"How do we walk out there again?" I asked, not looking at him.

"We just do," Jonis said. "Or I do, Lizzy. And if you're with me, then you do, too."

By the time we paid for the balloons and re-entered

the parking lot, the boys were gone. They hadn't wanted to face us again either.

Back at my apartment, we sat on the floor in the living room. Inka's cheeks were flushed and with every balloon she inflated she chanted, "I'm going to pass out!" then grabbed a fresh balloon from the package, stretched it, and started blowing again.

"Stop whining. We're doing this for you," I said.

Inka rolled her eyes childishly. "We're doing it for Carl. And if you don't want to then I'll do it all myself and you'll find me dead here by tomorrow."

"We should have bought a pump," I said. "In fact, couldn't we still?"

"Where's the fun in that?" Jonis asked.

Inka cackled. Her laugh was far too loud. She sat hunched forward, her meaty breasts hanging out of her tank top, and her hair pulled messily into a side ponytail. I had agreed two weeks prior to help Inka with this project. That was before she had betrayed me.

"Have you ever had short hair?" I asked Inka.

"What are you saying?"

"I'm saying you might try short hair."

"I shaved my head once in fifth grade," Jonis offered. "It was awkward."

I pictured him bald, his pointy ears sticking out, his chin sharp, his eyes forthright instead of hidden by falling brown strands.

"An army boy," Inka stated.

"He couldn't be an army boy," I said.

"Did somebody take their mean pills this morning?" Inka asked. She looked at Jonis. He looked at me. I stuck a red balloon in my mouth and starting blowing on it, my palm against the back so I could feel the rubber thinning out. I pushed more air and more, to stop myself from crying.

"Carl's turning 30," Inka said. "He's the oldest boy I've ever fucked."

"Man?" Jonis asked. "Isn't he a man?"

I tied my red balloon. I grabbed another from the bag.

"What kind of medicine will he practice?" Jonis asked. Jonis sat so straight on the floor, his good leg bent in like a triangle and the other extended out ending in a bag. It was the most comfortable place for him, better than any sofa or bed. On the floor there was infinite space, there was nothing to fall off of, no unevenness or give.

"He wants a pediatric practice, though I don't know that he'll be especially good with kids. His humor is dry and vulgar."

Inka talked of Carl like she knew everything about him, like she loved him, but Inka didn't believe in love. She said that commitment was love, that only after years of faithfulness and sacrifice could one claim to love another. She made it sound horrible, a condition no one would want to suffer.

"I had some pretty serious doctors as a kid. And I had doctors who tried too hard to be funny so that it ended up they were talking down to you and you had to do all the work pretending to be amused. Some of the boys were harder on the doctors than I was. They'd glare them down instead of pretending to laugh. Sometimes a serious doctor is better."

"I don't think he'll be working with children with real illnesses like yours, just, you know, the normal things: coughs, colds, chicken pox."

I added the last bit of air to my current balloon and it burst in a thick, loud "POP!" I held on to my ears as they rang with it.

"Don't put so much air," Inka suggested.

"They're cheap," I replied.

"Chill! What are you so stressed about?" Inka asked.

"Nothing. What are *you* so stressed about?" I regretted the question immediately, and I awaited Inka's long-winded response detailing all the things that were and had ever been wrong in her life.

"I'm not stressed – I'm happy!" Inka said, with too much emphasis on the 'ha.'

And she was. It was funny but amidst my anger and the valiant force I was using to hold it back, I hadn't noticed. This was the longest exclusive relationship Inka had been in since middle school, and really, who could count middle school? He would be wealthy, a doctor; I'm sure she liked that. There I had been thinking that Inka was really only dating Carl because I had started seeing Jonis and she wanted to show me up, or prove to me that she could leave me too. Perhaps it had started out as spiteful; perhaps all love did. I opened up to Jonis because I was neglected by Joe. Maybe the nature of connection was horrible, vengeful, a necessary rebellion against our natural closed state where no one and nothing can infiltrate our fear of the unknown.

"I'm starving. Let's order Chinese. What do you guys want? Ribs, lo mein, fried rice, some wonton soup, pot stickers, what else?" Inka asked.

"Isn't that enough?" Jonis thought of food like a chore.

"Lizzy and I usually account for two dinners worth of Chinese food, and if after two nights there's still a little extra we have it for lunch on the third day. An old habit from *Cheap College Living* – that's a magazine we invented sophomore year."

"We published and distributed two issues to our entire dorm," I said.

"Innovative ideas, like how making out with random boys at bars can save you around three thousand dollars a year on alcohol. You get it? Cheap has two meanings," Inka explained. "Inexpensive and sleazy."

"Aren't those the same?" Jonis asked.

"Oh, don't worry … Lizzy always had a boyfriend. She never got a chance to try the theories out like I did. Always missing out on the fun. "

Inka patted me hard on the back, and as if she'd burped it out of me, I blurted, "I'm leaving in two days."

"What? Where?" Inka and Jonis chorused.

"Joe," I said, and then I looked at Jonis to clarify, "my college ex-boyfriend…"

"A *very* distant ex," Inka added as if the air were not tense enough already.

"He's gotten me a gig performing in the city. It's a classical series for low-income schools and communities. The New York City Opera organized it. It's only for two weeks."

"That's wonderful!" Jonis said so convincingly that I almost believed him.

"I'm sorry. I should have told you sooner but I only just found out and I hadn't made up my mind yet."

"Of course you have to do it," Jonis said.

Inka pursed her lips, with jealousy or contempt. We had not discussed the fact that she had told Joe about Jonis. With Inka it was hard to tell if she was waiting for the scene I might make or if she'd already forgotten all about it.

"So that's what all this grumpiness has been about." She paused. "Don't worry, dear. We'll get on without you for two weeks. Won't we, Jonis?"

Jonis nodded, unsure.

Inka wedged a thin knife under the window and gave it a pry. It came up easily. She hoisted me up towards the ledge to take off the screen and then hoisted me further so that I could climb through. I pulled at my weight and shimmied against the windowsill until I had one knee over and could pull the rest of myself in. It was strange to break into an unfamiliar house.

Carl's dark bedroom smelled of sandalwood, his cologne or recently lit incense? I ran my hands up and down the walls until I found a light and though Inka assured me that Carl was out, I made a quick check of the surroundings to be sure that Carl wouldn't pop out of the bed or a closet in defense against the intruder. He was the kind of boy who could take a girl down.

"Go unlock the door," Inka called from outside.

I made my way through the apartment, tidy and small with hardwood floors and newly painted walls, and unlocked the front door. Outside, I could see Jonis in his car, the glow of the interior lights made his pale face visible in pieces, a nose, a cheek. The bass of his music boomed and the balloons moved to the beat, bumping all around him.

Inka and I took out the balloons that filled Jonis's car, then we emptied my car, followed by Inka's. The balloons filled Carl's room with their assorted colors. Inka took out one balloon and taped it to Carl's front door. She wrote on it with a sharpie: *Happy Birthday, Carl My Love!* And she stood for a moment to admire it.

I couldn't imagine that Carl would be very happy upon seeing so many balloons littering his room. He might shuffle them around for a moment and then fall into bed or pop them one by one, sweep up the mess, and return his apartment to its previous neatness. But Inka was proud of our efforts, as if such an abundance of balloons certainly denoted love.

CHAPTER THIRTEEN

The cool air of November freed the city, pushing wind between buildings and across streets. The pollution floated up beyond the skyscrapers and the scent of roasted peanuts and frying hot dogs gently touched the nose before escaping. Joe and I walked down long numbered blocks towards the theater, and I asked him of each one, "Will it ever end?" The early morning sun patted our backs as we hopped in and out of shadows. "Soon!" Joe assured me. He was rosy-cheeked and giddy, so in love with the life he was leading.

Before the turn of our last corner, Joe stopped us mid-stride and caught a bobby pin that was hanging from my hair. He pushed it back in hard so that it hit my scalp. He reached out and took my hand. "You look beautiful like this," he said.

Joe and I had gone shopping together the day before to pick out my attire. I settled on this gray skirt suit with three black buttons on the front. One of Joe's housemates, Barbara, helped to fasten my hair into a tight French twist and urged me to put on more makeup.

"I don't know why I'm doing all this," I said.

"Because making a good first impression on Don

Bartley can have endless positive effects for a musician. He is connected, kind, and so beloved at the Opera. If he likes you it could turn your whole career around."

I wanted to remind him that he was the one with the career, not I. But I was trying hard to be on good behavior, to have a pleasant time despite the constant churning in my stomach.

Barbara had been in the City Opera chorus as a soprano for twenty-three years. She always lived in small city apartments with roommates from the chorus. She always wore her hair pulled back tightly. She told me, secretively, that she knew Joe would be a soloist someday soon, that he would stand in front and command the whole stage. The secret made her giggle. "We're lucky to know him," she said.

The newly renovated Lincoln Center was wide and impressive like an old cultured woman dressed in jewels. I had been there as a child to hear an orchestra with my parents and I could still conjure that sense of pure grandeur. I had wanted instantly to inhabit it, like Annie in Daddy Warbucks' mansion, sliding down the banisters, and running through the marble-floored halls. The trip was for my birthday and we had arrived early and sat outside by the fountains, throwing in pennies for good luck. I was wearing a black velvet dress with patent leather shoes, buckles across the front. My mother told me to repeat the conductor's name so that I might remember it: Kurt Masur, Kurt Masur. Her voice descending *G sharp*, *F sharp*, *E*, with each syllable. I repeated it in her tones and bobbed my head to the song of them.

I loved the sound of the orchestra tuning up to pitch, the stopping and starting of winds, the squawking and stroking of bows, but when Mozart's piano concertos began I was overcome with frustration. I had listened to the piece with my parents the week before, in the living room, after dinner, and it had been different then. The pitch was higher now than it had been on the recording, the tempo was quicker. I could hear the recorded version in my mind, clashing along with the current version being performed in front of me. The noise was painful, infuriating. I began to cry for I couldn't turn either version off. I cried so loudly that my mother had to take me out of the hall.

I spent most of the concert in the bathroom, a lovely bathroom with velvet pink sofas. "I want a bedroom that looks like this someday," I told my mom, and she rolled her eyes. I suggested we play tea party rather than sit around and do nothing and she complied. I told people we'd had a wonderful time at the concert, though my parents never did take me back to Lincoln Center. I didn't return, in fact, until Inka and I saw Joe in *Carmen*, his first production with City Opera. Now, they were rehearsing for *Candide*, long tedious rehearsals, 10 AM to 8 PM.

"You'll like *Candide*," Joe told me as we entered. "Voltaire, a play within a play … have you read it?"

I nodded. "Have *you*?"

He shrugged. "I know enough about it now. You'll have to come back and see it when we start. I'm on stage like the whole time."

Joe took me to a back corridor of offices. He introduced me to the music director from the Opera who was running the "Looking Forward" series. Don Bartley was a square-headed stuffy man with a big warm belly laugh. He was the one I had dressed to impress.

"Happy to have you," he said. "I admire musicians who donate their time."

I reached out and gave him my firmest of handshakes.

I was afraid he'd ask for a copy of the meager resume I had printed up, or inquire as to what I was working on at the moment, but he didn't seem to be at all interested in me or my credentials.

"You can come to the rehearsals tomorrow and Wednesday, I hope. We've had this theater intern standing in on piano and, well, I don't have to tell you … anyway, we're happy to have you. Joe tells us good things."

With that he dismissed me.

I wondered what Joe had told them. How had he presented me? A good musician he knew? His girlfriend? Or just a friend, an acquaintance, a woman blandly associated.

There was a dark-haired woman standing before me when I turned around. She had wide, tear-shaped eyes, the drop of the tear pointing in towards her nose.

"So this is her," she said to Joe. "She's very pretty."

She reached out her hand to me and took it with an eyebrow shift. She was all decked out with thick eyeliner and rouge. I imagined her in my scene, where Joe calls me from the bathroom after leaving the bed of a beautiful woman, and I nodded, yes, this would be the woman he was sleeping with.

"Joe describes you as kind, so I didn't know you'd be good-looking. It's always interesting to know how you're portrayed by others, no?" Her voice was dense, an operatic tone. She'd sing with all that dark "woo-ooo-ing," lifting the throat right out of the body. I wasn't fond of the operatic tone. I preferred the straight airy choral voice for its purity and exactness.

"It's interesting to see who he's portraying me to," I replied.

"Oh, you're a heart-breaker," she said like she was some kind of gypsy reading my fortune. "Only certain girls can truly break a heart."

We were flooded then by a group of opera members. Joe threw out some names as introductions then led me to a section of the theater where I could watch the rehearsal. He pressed his apartment key into my palm, "Watch for however long you like," he said, and looked as if he wished he could say something more, something to combat what the dark-haired woman had divulged, but in the end he came up with only, "Wait till you see me dance!"

Before long the group was singing. It was strange to hear an opera in English. The voices were luxuriously blended, straighter than most opera sounds. It felt more like a musical, and perhaps it was. Maybe in the language of English there was no way to keep the opera firmly fixed. The songs were not tragic but rather pining. They were every bit Bernstein. I recalled playing one of the songs from this opera *Make My Garden Grow* with a small performing group during college. What a melody! And it's simple refrain, "And I will try, before I die, to make some sense of life…" I envied singers their tools, the ability to express words and sounds together. They could even gesture or dance. As an instrumentalist I had only the pitch and beat and somehow they were not enough. I closed my eyes to pick Joe's voice out from the rest. I found and followed it. I had missed his voice.

The director cut in, "Fine! Fine. Moving on…" They were staging now and Joe moved from place to place. He was both more slender and more muscular than he had been the last time I'd seen him more than three months before. His arms floated by his sides like ropes, his legs had a light, almost gay scamper. He must have been training hard, several dance classes a week. He probably did yoga. My strong reserved Joe had become a man of the theater. He was nothing of the awkward boy I had fallen for in choir rehearsal, mortified to blush from a bit of Dalcroze. Joe began to move elegantly, stage right to stage left. He looked out into the audience and unabashedly winked at me. I felt my feet begin to shake, my hands, my neck. I was cold or I was about to cry.

The following day, at my first "Looking Forward" rehearsal, I was rhythmic and precise, which worked well for ensembles, especially those not privy to ample rehearsal time. There was a quartet and a small singing group of maybe fifteen, me on the piano, and a tall slender gentleman on percussion. Bartley stopped in and offered me his nod of approval. His nod felt nice. Being a piece of something larger, however impermanent, felt nicer.

Joe sang during all the numbers that required voice. There was a dance section during the Debussy piece, a ballet number that Joe, to my relief, did not partake in. There was a propless scene enacted of *Carmen* in which Joe sang one of the solo roles beautifully. This was nothing, I knew, a show for high schools and under-funded community centers, but as I listened to Joe singing I knew that what Barbara said was right. He would soon come into his tenor voice completely, and he would hold the stage for years.

Now, finally, Joe and I had some time together. We ate kettle corn on the small sofa in his room.

"So what'd you think of it all?" Joe asked.

"I was nervous," I said.

The room was square and white-walled, newly renovated or at least freshly painted. It was just large enough to fit his bed, loveseat, TV, and a small dresser, but it had its own adjoining bathroom; each of the bedrooms did. Barbara, who had eaten a pizza dinner with us in the kitchen, said this was her favorite feature of the place. "There's nothing like having your own bathroom!"

I had expected that over the course of the year Joe would have found a more age-appropriate roommate, someone not old enough to be his mother. I thought he'd move in with his band, a four-man rock-folk group who shared a hovel on the Lower East Side, but he hadn't and didn't now mention any intention of doing so. He seemed perfectly contented, in every way.

"There's something I have to tell you," Joe said. "I should have told you."

"Really, Joe. I'd rather not hear it. I'd rather not do this whole big confession thing. Let's just leave it, okay? I'm here. You're here. Let's enjoy each other's company. Soon I'll be gone."

I didn't want to hear about his affairs. It would simply ruin our two weeks if I had to face him and his fuck buddy every day of the show and then sleep there on the blow up bed on his bedroom floor every night imagining them together. It seemed obvious to me that we should let the past stay in the past, but Joe looked hurt, almost stunned. He put his hands on my knees, such perfect strong hands.

"We were together for almost four years," he said.

"Four years," I repeated. "An impossibly long time."

Everything had been different four years before. I had a perfect family. I was still a child.

"I don't want to talk about who I have or haven't been sleeping with, Lizzy. What I need you to know is why I didn't ask you to move here with me."

I relaxed. "Go ahead."

"I wanted to start this life alone. It would have been easy for me to live in an apartment with you, to hook up on weekends with our other friends in the area, to eat dinner together every night. I would have loved it, I swear. But I needed to force myself into a totally new kind of life. I needed to make friends and take dance classes and find a band. I needed to spend every night in rehearsal rooms working my voice. I needed not to be judged by anyone or helped by anyone or needed by anyone. I've never done that before. I've never been alone and if I didn't do this, I was afraid I'd have regretted it my whole life. I'd have taken it out on you years from now, when we were retired and our children grown. I'd have wished there had been a time when it was just me and the world and my music."

Joe looked up. His eyes were teary and he looked hurt to see that mine were not. "I should have told you. I should have been straight with you. I should have called you more, visited more, so much more. I didn't think I'd lose you, Lizzy. I was arrogant. I'm so sorry."

I put my forehead to his so I wouldn't have to look at him. I remembered our visions of being old together, starting an "old timers' band" and touring the world. I had shared unburdened time with Joe, when it still seemed realistic to believe in a future where things worked out as you planned them, and where absolute happiness was possible – a time before I worried about having a career or about the inevitability of my parent's growing apart and old. I thought of recreating that feeling, of reaching back for it. I thought of staying, of pursuing. I thought of a workshop I'd taken in college entitled *How to Make a Living as a Professional Musician*. They told us to go out into the community and make ourselves known. Become acquainted with school systems so that they will hire you for their shows and recommend you as a private lesson instructor to their students. Start small community music groups, even if not the caliber you'd prefer, local musicians can help connect you to other opportunities. Practice often and audition often so that the next gig doesn't ever seem out of reach or impossible. Joe had done it all. All the things we were supposed to do. I made to move my forehead off of his forehead, but Joe reached his hand behind my hair and gently held my neck in place. His hand was warm and filled me with a comfort I no longer believed in.

Movement III

The field shimmering with flowers,
The stars swirling in the heavens,
The song of the lark
Fills the blue abyss.

Apollon Maykov ("Song of the Lark")

CHAPTER FOURTEEN

Jonis was pale. The sheets were pale. The moonlight crept in slanting rows onto his bed and across his face. A mosaic of dust fluttered across the contraptions he was connected to: an IV, a series of raised blocks keeping the entirety of his leg strapped and elevated. His leg, covered by thin white sheets, lay across tables that had been pulled together to cross from one side to the other of his private room. I had never seen anyone I loved so completely unfurled.

"He must be cold," I said and I rushed to a stack of blue blankets and covered Jonis's leg with them piece by piece. Patty nodded and let me continue. I wasn't sure she approved, but I couldn't bear the idea that anyone who walked into this room would see him like this. I smoothed out the creases in the blankets and stood back to admire my work. Patty took my hand and squeezed it briefly. We stood together and waited, she in her sweat suit and I in my emerald gown.

Jonis's eyes twitched and then opened.

Patty rushed towards him and I stepped politely away; my heels clicked aggressively on the linoleum. I looked out the window, to avoid the intimacy of the moment; gray clouds swirled around the newly waxing moon, expanding and receding like breath.

"Jonis…" Patty said softly, a comfort. "We're here."

Jonis scrambled his hands out from under the blanket as if they were suffocating.

"Lizzy?" he asked.

Summoned, I stepped forward.

"I saw your mother," Jonis said to me. He talked in a whisper. Jonis tried to push himself up but his arms didn't seem able to support his shoulders, nor his neck able to support his head. He retreated back into the pillow.

Patty placed her palms on his shoulders. "Rest now."

"I have to tell you," he said. His eyes were wide. "I feel like I'm melting, not away but like rain, melting down to the soil. I keep asking you if you can see it. Lizzy, can you see me melting?"

I looked at Patty, frightened.

"Don't worry," Patty laughed. "Even the sanest among us sounds this way on morphine."

"Lizzy?" Jonis asked again. "Are you listening?"

I leaned my elbows on his bed and tilted my face in towards him, to assure him that I was listening. His eyes softened and then closed; his mouth moved around a few syllables growing less comprehensible and less audible until there was nothing left but the movement, and then nothing left at all. He fell back into the dream he'd popped out of only he was less peaceful, his mind jittery and resistant, not quite giving in to the drugs, the rest his body required of him.

It had been five minutes to seven when I received the call from Patty, her voice evenly pitched. "A series of blood clots," she said. "He'll be fine, but I thought that you'd want to know." There was a fluctuation in her last three words, a rising pitch where there should have been a fall. Jonis had been rushed to Ithaca's Cayuga Hospital, stabilized with medication, and then driven down to the city in an ambulance to the Children's Hospital. The Bronx's local theater sported echoing ceilings above the musty curtain. I could feel the vibrations of all the voices pummeling down upon me as I stood behind the stage. This, our last performance, was to begin in a few minutes.

"I can be there in under an hour," I said.

I smoothed my hands on my green pleated dress and clenched my whole body into a wish that I would be allowed to complete this last show.

"He's having a filter put into the leg to keep the clot from moving to his lungs. Don't rush. Finish your performance. You can't be of any help to him until he's out of surgery, anyway. You're so close," Patty said. "I wish I could come hear you. I really do."

I hadn't expected that that would be her wish and I felt guilty for my own.

I shut the phone, put it into my bag, and took a drink of water before walking out into the theater with the two other instrumentalists and the percussionist. The crowd applauded as I adjusted myself on the piano bench and stretched my fingers. Then a silence came over them, a lovely anticipation that held until the violinist took his preparatory breath and brought us all in. I pushed my fingers over the keys and as they depressed I could hear the fluctuation of pitch before it settled. I did not love performing, but it was nice to be a part of this emanating sound, to possess the power to alter it. Tuning pianos was solitary. When I set the strings I was proud, but there was never any applause.

The performers made their entrances, and my arms stiffened. I rushed and then caught myself and settled back into time. Joe danced across the stage and Jonis was cut open, his fragile systems altered. I felt Jonis there amidst the notes, as if in this last performance he had entered the ensemble. I could sense his suffering and it mixed with the music like a new kind of sound, a low booming; it built, it steadied, and soon I could hear his crutching rhythm approaching from behind. It was unmistakable: step, click, step, click. I had to tense my neck to keep from turning. *He's not there*, I told myself. It was a trick. I couldn't give in to it – I didn't want to turn, like Orpheus, to stone.

I wondered if he could hear me, too, a melody to his induced sleep. I imagined the chorus gathered around his hospital bed: "You've ruined us!" their voices called out all at once, and then they silenced. The dancers exited. The soloist stepped forward. My fingers lingered above the keys as the soprano's airy *F* signaled the start to "Un bel di vedremo," the beautiful aria from *Madame Butterfly*. His crutching rhythm had stopped. I worried that he had left me. I imagined what kind of call I might receive, how I would crumple to the floor, how Joe would pick me up but wouldn't be able to hold me for long. I began to play. I kept my eyes affixed to the notes on the page, afraid of all peripheral space, afraid I'd see an image of him, a ghostly image, similar to the one I now found in the hospital bed before me.

It was a half-hour before he came to again. He was considerably more composed and spent a few minutes consulting with Patty about the details of the procedure he'd undergone. She told him what she knew and then set off to find a doctor to fill him in on the rest. Jonis and I were finally alone.

"Look at me," he said. "In the '40s, I would have joined the circus, the freak show." His voice chipped. He cleared his throat.

I sat down by his side and took hold of his hand. I tossed it about like a hot muffin.

"You look beautiful," Jonis said. "Was it wonderful?"

I nodded. It *had* been wonderful.

"It…" I began, but in this sterile room the details of my thrilling adventures would be cruel. "It was nice to be part of it again, but I missed you."

My eyes darted from cloth chair to TV set, unable to make contact. I teetered back and forth from the desire I had built up after being away from Jonis for two weeks, and the idea that a man in a hospital bed cannot be desired. I hesitated and then gently leaned in to him for a kiss. He pulled me tightly to him and I shuddered in his arms as our tongues lapped each other slowly. He felt too thin. I wanted more of him.

"I've never performed on a stage," Jonis said.

Time was on his mind. It was also on mine. Nearly midnight. The others were likely at a bar by now, dancing sloppily, taking shots of Jack Daniel's and starting to forget me. Joe looked so handsome when he hugged me goodbye, and in that moment I *had* been beautiful whereas here in the hospital I knew how ridiculous I looked in my shiny green dress.

"In elementary school we had four tiers of risers for our music shows, and I had to sit beside the risers in a chair," Jonis continued.

"There will be plenty of time for stages," I told him. "Maybe we'll put one in our house someday so we can sit on it all alone and play for no one."

After I suggested it, the idea immediately lost its enchantment. I pictured a house of dark wood and dimmed lights, the accursed abode of Rigoletto. Upon a dank stage, I would sit and play lonely ballads to an empty room.

"We'll have to teach you something to play," I said.

"I could always go back to the recorder." Jonis shifted under the blankets. "Where should our house be?" he asked. "Somewhere expansive … the edge of an ocean."

I thought of it, the blue easily picturesque, the cold wind. It might infuriate me. You couldn't do anything on the east-coast ocean, couldn't swim but two months a year, couldn't canoe or skate. You could only stare out at its distant horizon, so easy to see and so impossible to reach. I knew what the ocean was to him. It was openness. It was possibility. He didn't think of water skiing or ice skating;

he'd never done these things, but I wanted him to. I wanted the whole world before him, not off in the distance, not to be observed or longed for.

"No," I said firmly.

Jonis laughed. His eyes fanned out with creases over his taught, dry skin, which I stroked with my fingers.

"I had no idea you were anti-ocean. A river then?" Jonis asked.

"A lake," I said.

"But seriously, I have to tell you about this hallucination I had," Jonis said.

"I'm surprised you remember…"

"Yes," he said. "Every detail."

He sat up slowly and successfully and I put a few pillows behind his back to support him. He prepared with a breath in which his face drew with color and life.

"I walk down a tilting road. You're pulling me, saying 'Come on, come on,' as if I'm standing still. But I swear I'm moving. My body is floppy and slow, but it's moving. More swimming than walking, it's the strangest sensation, smooth like a deep inhalation – that part where the lungs are satisfied, everything rests, and all the thoughts call out at once but you don't mind them. Like when you're totally yourself.

"I realize that my leg is trailing behind me, like way behind, possibly not attached to me, and that's what you mean. That's why you keep telling me to hurry, to come on, because I'm moving but my leg isn't. I swim back to my leg and start pounding at it like I'm trying to wake it up. I consider tearing it off like Velcro but then I hear a lulling voice, the sound of an old friend, Doug, coaxing me into my first drug trip. 'It's a poison,' he says, 'being released in your body. It's all coming out of you. In the end you're free.' But I know, even at that moment, that it can't be Doug. Doug is in Syracuse, sick in bed with hepatitis. Doug disappears and I look around and you're gone too. I'm alone on this weird water-road. At this point

I realize that I'm in surgery, that I must be full of drugs."

"Has that ever happened to you before?" I asked.

"Not that I can remember. It's strange, almost like I've come out and can really see the room I'm in, the people there with me. The image of Dr. Kershner standing above me expands and fades like a firework. I want him to know that I can see him incase this will be a problem, so I call out, 'I can't take it.' And someone answers, 'It will pass like a stomach ache.'"

"Really?"

"No … I don't know. I doubt that I really called anything out. I doubt that someone answered. The voice is strange. It doesn't seem to be female or male and for some reason I think the 'it' being referred to is love. That love for anything can pass like a stomach ache if you just let it go. I feel comforted by this idea and by knowing that Dr. Kershner is there with me.

"I hear a series of beeps. They start out steady like a life-support machine, but then they accelerate and become a phone ringing. I answer and it's your Mom. I know her voice immediately, though we've never met. She says hi to me. She says she knows where I am. I want to acknowledge her, but it occurs to me that I don't know her first name…"

"It's Gayle."

"I didn't know. You've never said."

"I suppose it hasn't come up."

"'Mrs. Schwartz?' I say to her, because that's all I know to call her. She tells me that she's in the library. She wants to know the name of a book that I read years ago. I try but I can't tell her the title because I don't remember it. 'I can't talk to you now, under these conditions,' I tell her. 'What's wrong with you? Are you all right? Are you safe?' she asks. 'I don't remember,' I say. 'There was this line. I need to read it again. It made me feel okay about my life. I need that line,' she says. 'I'm sorry,' I say, 'but I don't know you at all.'

"There's a window. I look through it and I see her, your mother. She charges down the road in a long black jacket. Her remorse washes over me like the light of a projector when you stand in front of it, and I try to dodge it, to the left and to the right, but it keeps up; it catches me. She's crying. Her tears are cold and I feel her tears like I *am* the tears, like I'm gathering and pressing out of her tear ducts and falling to the earth. It happens again and again, I gather and I fall. I'm afraid that I'll be trapped in this cycle forever, full of sadness."

"I'll bring you to meet her," I said apologetically, because we both knew I'd been hiding him.

Jonis had tears in his own eyes and wiped them away as a doctor entered, Patty trailing behind him. I wished I could escape before the doctor noticed my dress, before I had to hear any negative results or watch a physician coolly scan Jonis's body for signs of ailment or harm. I didn't want to respond to Jonis's vision or to be trapped any longer in that room. Sickness was not meant for new love, a hole in the façade. The doctor hid his face behind a chart and then pulled the chart away.

"Look who I found," Patty announced.

"Petey?" Jonis asked in a high throaty whisper. "Shit! A doctor."

"Oh god, it's so good to see you," Petey said.

Petey nodded his head in small bobs and smiled from his eyes. He gave Jonis a rambunctious handshake, holding on too long. If Jonis were standing I imagined he would have pulled him into an embrace.

"Surgeon, actually," Petey said. "I was doing residency in Cambodia, came back into the country a few months ago, and here I am."

"You're just like me," Jonis said. "A glutton for this place."

Petey looked over at Jonis's leg as if to say *it's still there*. He asked, "What are you in for?"

"Blood clot," Jonis waved his hand to dismiss the

steady, heavy syllables.

Petey was a classically handsome man: the tall, dark stranger; the somewhat sympathetic villain. I watched him with cockeyed interest, a bird staring out of its cage at the activity of the world. Jonis introduced me as his girlfriend and I strained to think if he had he ever said this before out loud to anyone other than me. Petey shook my hand in a professional way and told me forthrightly that he and Jonis had been in the hospital together as children.

"I was a 'burn child,'" he said, and I knew him then. A young boy covered in scars suffering surgery after surgery, to correct the tattered skin, to pull it back to normal. Misfit friends, probably running through the wards burping the alphabet and wondering about the nature of transformation. Outwardly, now, Petey had no signs of burns; of course I could only see his face and his hands, but his earnest grip on his clipboard, the way he held Jonis's gaze pleading for a chance to fix him, let me know that on the inside he had been changed by the time spent in hospital gowns, gauzed and waiting for his chance at "real life."

"You ever see anything when you were in surgery?" Jonis asked Petey. "Like a vision?"

"I heard music once," Petey said. "It started and then I had no way to stop it. It was everywhere with no pause. It was very tangible, too. It had tastes and scents and it pressed on me like something material, like a wet blanket on my skin or a slice of bread with too much butter in my mouth. I couldn't hear it or feel it anymore when I woke up, but I remembered it. I was seventeen and for a few years after I listened to a lot of classical music. My mom thought it was weird; it creeped her out. I kept wanting to find something that sounded like that music, but I've never heard anything like it."

"What do you think it means?" Jonis asked.

Petey laughed. "I remember that about you." He took a brief glance around the room to see that things were in order. "I'll send your surgeon in but I'll stop by again later for some more catching up."

"Why didn't you do my surgery, man?" Jonis said. "You holding out on me?"

Petey patted him on the shoulder, said, "Maybe next time," and whisked away into the white hallway where the wheels of patients in transit could be heard murmuring like hungry stomachs as the calls and clicking clipboards of nurses chorused on.

"He's too young to be a surgeon," Patty said.

"Not everyone younger than you is *too young* anymore, Mom."

"You used to tell me that you loved me when you came out of surgery," she said. "Your words all slurred like a drunk old man: 'I luuuuuuve you, mooooooommy...' I miss those days."

I cracked a window open behind us to let in some air. I took a brief pause to check that my mother wasn't truly out there somewhere, crying, looking for me and wondering, like all mothers do, when I'd be home.

CHAPTER FIFTEEN

The afternoon he was discharged, Jonis met Petey for lunch in Hoboken, New Jersey, at a gourmet pizza place with a view of the Hudson. The sky was dark as dusk, thunder and lightening threatened but did not give way to rain, leaving the air, and everyone it touched, heavy. Some 200 miles away, I experienced the same dark humidity; the looming storm spread strong across the tristate area, maybe even the whole east coast, the winds, the tides, the push and pull of particles, all in sync, so that for a brief moment one might comprehend the connectedness of all.

I cleaned up from my journey with laundry, list making, and some dusting, to distract myself from the phone that was not ringing with Joe's lust and the door that was not opening with Jonis's return, as Jonis and Petey sat in a dimly lit corner near the back of the restaurant with a candle between them.

"They say candlelight during meals can relax you and improve digestion," Petey said. He was dressed casually, jeans and a t-shirt, which sat awkwardly on him as if he hadn't worn this style in some time.

"I'll believe it if you do," Jonis replied. "It must be nice to know real things. My job is all about manipulation.

Marketing and sales is a guessing game. I like that about it, the creativity, but sometimes I'd like to *know*, not to *guess*. Facts."

It occurred to Jonis that he couldn't have been a doctor even if he'd wanted to. Maybe a biologist or scientist, but not a surgeon like Petey, not a person who made rounds in a hospital, dealt with patients, saved lives. He'd never encountered a deformed doctor. Doctors did not have crutches or wheelchairs or missing arms, bulbous tumors, cleft palates, scars. Jonis had never considered this obvious limitation before. He felt foolish to have accepted too much of his life as it was.

"Knowing isn't all it's cracked up to be," Petey said. "The more I find out about medicine, the stupider I feel. When I was younger I'd watch the doctors with complete awe. Their speech and their walks and their white jackets, it was all so sure and neat. Most people feel that way about actors, I guess. For me it was doctors and now that I am one, I don't know, it doesn't seem as great an achievement as I'd hoped it would be."

"It *is* great," Jonis said.

Petey had come far from the boy he remembered, angry and mischievous, the kind Jonis was drawn to at that time when the hospital was keeping him from the whole, great, exciting world. Petey had been three years older than Jonis, smart, daring, and crude. Petey's father would visit him in the hospital dirty from whatever odd job he was trying at the time, slurring drunk. That man made Jonis feel lucky that he'd never had a father to deal with. But Petey was good with him. He kept him in his place. He told him where the coffee was, he gave him stern glances when he got too loud and began to disturb the other patients.

"Is your old man still alive?" Jonis asked.

"Yeah, he's hanging in there. I forgave him, you know. After Marta and I got together and I finished my residency, I had this feeling that it was all because of him.

He was the thing I was fighting against, the driving force behind my desire to live a full life, to become a surgeon. You should see my scars. Twelve surgeries. I'll show you sometime. My arms look as good as any guy's, my back doesn't have the right texture when you touch it but to look at it you'd never know. I can wear a bathing suit. I can shower in men's locker room. I could take a girl home and not be treated like a freak."

The waiter came then and took their orders, took a moment too long trying to figure them out.

"Do you remember that night we tried to break into Dr. K's office?" Jonis asked.

Petey laughed. "What did we even want to get in there for?"

"To see our files, and to change them. We were going to write ourselves well."

"How about popcorn Tuesdays, that crappy microwave low-sodium stuff? Until we talked Dr. K into donating a real popcorn maker."

"I was there for a lot of popcorn Tuesdays after you left. That was good popcorn," Jonis said.

"I thought of going back to visit," Petey said. "I thought of calling you, but I never did."

"Doesn't matter," Jonis said.

"It matters, Jonis." Petey took a sip of his drink. "I was scared you'd still be sick when I'd gotten better. I was scared I'd find out that you had died and that I'd never recover from it. I decided I'd rather not know."

I imagine Petey looked scared, then. Doctors, friends, lovers, family, we are a whole society that doesn't talk about death. We don't ask questions that we don't want to hear the answers to. I had been with Jonis for over five months. I had seen him almost every day, but I hadn't asked him the questions that looped in my mind: "How long will you live for? Will you see your children grow up? Live to be a grandfather? What are the odds of time for you and me?"

"I don't want to be your savior or anything," Petey started, "but when you asked me here to dinner I decided that I was going to say this to you, so here it goes. I know Kershner never pushed you, either because of your mother or because he was scared of complications, but it's a good time now, Jonis: you're healthy, strong, you're still young but you're old enough to make this decision. To own it. To own your life. That's all I'll say about it. If you want to set up a consultation we can talk more, we can get started. Okay?" he said. "Now, let's get to nurse Miranda and how I fucked her."

"You did not!" Jonis laughed.

"I did. We were in a supplies closet. It was so cliché, so perfectly cliché."

At this point, Jonis must have slammed his hands onto the table, or leaned in real close like a betrayed lover and whispered, "Really?"

"I swear I've been waiting my whole life to tell you that, because you're the only one on this planet it could matter to as much as it mattered to me. I wanted so badly to tell you back then. You have no idea. But you were young and you loved her so purely and she loved you. If you'd have been older I never would have had a chance."

"Just once?" Jonis asked.

"Once. My first time. It was my third skin graft. I told all my friends back home about it and then I regretted it. They acted like she was any nurse. They wanted me to set them up so she could fuck them, too. But she wasn't any nurse. She was so much more. She was everything good and understanding, everything the world wasn't."

"I've had this fantasy, that I run into her on the street, walking…" Jonis started. "You know, I fantasize about walking. Right foot, left foot. I dream about what it used to feel like. What do you think that means?"

"Foreshadowing," Petey said, and then quickly, "I'm kidding. Who knows what any of it means? I've fantasized about running into her, too."

"She wouldn't like you now," Jonis said. "Too succ-
essful – there's nothing about you to save."

"Oh," Petey laughed, "there's always something to
save."

"So what was it like? No, don't tell me. No, do. Do
tell me."

"It was like you've imagined it. Or a little bit less perfect, but almost. We kissed for a while and then she asked
me if I wanted to. I was shy. She had to tell me what to do,
but she knew just what to tell me…"

"She wasn't just anyone," Jonis chorused.

"You'll forgive me?" Petey replied.

"I guess it's better that one of us got to have her."

Petey patted Jonis on the shoulder and the waiter
showed up with their meals. It seemed they'd gotten to
everything and so they ate quietly. The candlelight flicked
shadows across the small table so that sometimes when
they looked at each other they could be confused for the
boys they once were.

CHAPTER SIXTEEN

The pages of the local phone book were coarse and rippled from being left out on my patio for months. I had taken it in to recycle it but found myself flicking through in search of inspiration.

"We could go out for wings…" I suggested.

"I don't feel like that," Jonis called from the living room.

"Pizza?"

"I told you I had pizza for lunch, with my mother. Weren't you listening?"

"Right," I replied. "I forgot."

In fact I had remembered. I only wanted to see if he would. I went back to the yellow pages.

"Is this the onset of our stasis?" Jonis asked dramatically.

He was sprawled across the livingroom floor scanning channels so that every few seconds a completely different kind of noise came spewing out. I heard Inka huffing from behind her closed door. The night before she'd demanded complete silence from the hours of eight to midnight so that she could "concentrate on her work." In all our time together I had never seen her bring office work home.

"A movie?" I asked. "Bowling? Have you had those?"

"Bowling?" he questioned.

I should have known better but I wasn't always thinking. I wasn't and could never be accustomed to his limitations. "You could use that kiddy slope. The ball rolls right down!"

I could sense a smile in Jonis's silence and I was tempted to, but didn't add, that I had used this technique once in eighth grade when I'd broken my leg in two places. I had only once spoken to him of that four-month period during which I was on crutches. I spoke to the pains on the underarms and the claustrophobic sensation of being contained in a cast. "I had all these dreams that I was trapped in a box and couldn't get out," I had said. Jonis looked at me with the pain of years in which others empathized, imagined, explained in what ways they were like him – they could understand. I can say that I hadn't meant it this way, but I had. We all try to relate.

"I could have more pizza," he said. "If you want pizza, my Java bird." He came across from the living room carefully, wincing as he stepped. I took chunks of the phone book between my fingers and dropped them down onto the rest to hear the muffled thump of their contact.

"I'm not going to make you eat the same thing twice in one day," I said. "Where'd you go?"

"Sammy's… We could go someplace else. I could order something else. Eggplant parm?"

I knew he was lying. It all added up. The slow pace at which he moved from living room to kitchen, that odd tempo delay which made his rhythm foreign to me, a re-mix. His pale complexion and the obvious fact that when I called him at the office that afternoon he had been missing. "Out all day on some errand," Patty said. "Boys all have their mysteries."

I wasn't sure where he had been and I didn't really care, but the fact that he was keeping something from me made me uneasy. My stomach felt tight. Suddenly, I had lost my appetite.

"How about we skip dinner and get candy and popcorn at the movies instead," I suggested.

"Good," Jonis said.

I called to Inka to ask if she would like to come, though she never did want to join us on outings. She had a plethora of vague excuses: tired, busy, sick; twice in the past week she had been too "frazzled" to join us in the kitchen for dinner. She had developed a haunting look — an inhalation through the nostrils and lifting of the bottom lip. It was a warning. "My little Lizzy," the look claimed, "if you keep it up with this man he will destroy us." I tried my best to ignore it.

We entered the local independent theater through a narrow alleyway. That was Jonis's favorite part about it, that it was discreet instead of flashy with neon blinking signs. The feature we had chosen had something to do with shark fishing and that was about all we knew. We argued less in the choosing and during the discussions afterward when we went to see films that neither of us had investments in.

The theater was crowded and Jonis sighed as we looked around for an appropriate seat. Jonis had to sit at the end of the row so that he'd have enough room to extend out his leg. Most of the rows ends were taken up.

"Over there?" I asked, pointing to the front left.

"You'll never see over that guy's head."

"There?" I asked, pointing back a bit further.

Jonis nodded and started over down the aisle. Once he'd settled into his seat he handed me his crutches. I placed them on the floor beneath me and by the time I was finished Jonis's eyes were closed, his hands folded across his lap. I brushed my hand over his forehead: it was clammy and cold. I nudged him in the shoulder with my elbow.

"How long will you keep this up?" I asked. He was taking Vicodin every few hours to combat the pain he'd been having since his surgery.

"I'm fine," he said. "I'm following my prescription."

"That's not what I asked. You plan to follow this prescription for the rest of your life?"

"You've never felt pain like this, so don't act like you understand."

In the past few weeks he had started to ask for pity. He had started manipulating, like Inka did, to get his way with me or to shut me down. I wondered if he was heading towards a breakdown of some kind and I wondered if he had experienced one before. The first months of a relationship were meant to be the happiest time, and I was beginning to feel gypped. It wasn't that I didn't believe in his pain – I did – I knew it was there and so did the doctors. But I didn't believe that it was so much worse than it had been the week before the surgery, or the week before that, when he was happy and charming and fun despite it.

"Okay," I said. "I'm just asking, okay?"

Jonis took my hand and the previews started. The bombardment of sound and touch together jittered me, and my hand clenched tight around Jonis's.

"Ouch," he whispered and then, "Open the Skittles."

I leaned my head to his and asked, "Is it my fault that you're miserable?"

"Christ!" Jonis said. He pulled his hand away from mine. He grabbed for the package of Skittles that sat in my lap and opened them himself. "Not everything is about you."

I shifted uncomfortably in my seat, leaning away from him, and the movie started. I thought of getting up and running out of the theater and into the street but the fact that he couldn't chase after me, that he could never catch up, grab for me, calm me down, made the whole drama seem useless.

Jonis and I returned home from the movies late that

evening. Jonis flipped through a few chapters from the Dalai Lama's book on enlightenment that he was obsessed with reading and re-reading, "in order," he said, "to understand the words behind the words." To me the writing was straight, and I told him so. He kept searching anyway as if there lay a secret within.

Before long Jonis was tired and we prepared for bed. With the Vicodin, Jonis fell asleep easily. His 'sickness' was having the opposite effect on me. I had been having trouble sleeping or perhaps it was that I was having trouble sleeping next to Jonis. I felt like I had at the start of our relationship, jittery by his side, unable to let go or shut down or to stop looking at him. Only, on those first few nights of our relationship I was tightly wrapped in Jonis's arms, drifting in and out of sleep and conversation along with him. Now, only I lay awake, with no one to whisper to or hold close.

Jonis slept peacefully on his back. He was a still sleeper. He'd learned from his leg to be this way, not to disturb it. I leaned in close to his face to check that he was still breathing. He seemed fragile, like anything might go wrong. I rolled to my side. To the right and to the left. I checked for his breathing again. I tried, as I used to as a child when I couldn't sleep, putting my pillow at the opposite side of the bed. But that didn't work either. I was afraid, at that end, that I'd roll over in my sleep and hurt Jonis's leg.

I turned back upright. I nudged my head into Jonis's shoulder and relaxed its weight onto him. His mouth opened and closed at the center like a baby bird, and I thought of Carlotta. It had been months since I'd seen her and I knew she was waiting. It was terrible to keep someone waiting. Or had she already given up? It's not that I wasn't working on her project. I tried and tried again to make a connection. I looked at pitch first, of course: Carlotta versus the peacocks. I looked at the increments that pitches dropped or rose in her speaking voice verses peacock calls, no connection or relation. I looked at the frequency in which certain pitches occurred in each case. I formed number sequences, codes, but still nothing to tie them. Carlotta didn't speak in any way that reminded me of a peacock, her voice was clear and loud as was the peacocks. That was something, but not much. I didn't have it in me to call her with that, a thing so benign, when she was waiting for proof to hold and use. She spoke flat while the birds were sharp. She switched pitches quickly while peacocks tended to meditate on one for a long period of time, trying it out once and then again a bit sharp and then again a bit sharper. I turned onto my back and held my eyes shut; they fluttered and vibrated. I imagined the peacocks sounds mixed with Carlotta's voice. Together, they had a strange effect: movement and stasis. They complimented each other. My eyes fought against my hold and popped opened again. It was useless. I would never sleep again! I burned with frustration. I was useless.

"Jonis, I'm going home," I said. I said it loud and twice to wake him.

"It's snowing," he mumbled from some sleepy place.

"Yes," I said. "It is snowing."

He was quiet and I thought he'd fallen back to sleep completely, but then, "Drive well," he said. "Text me when you get there."

I waited to see if he'd ask me why or if he'd show any sign of alarm. I'd certainly never left his house in the middle of the night before. But that wasn't his style.

I put on my jeans and stole a heavy sweatshirt from his closet. The thought of the cold caused me to move slow. I went to the bathroom. I had some water in the kitchen. I retied the laces on my sneakers. I went to shut off the kitchen light, to leave the main house dark and empty, and I caught sight of the spare office key that hung on its peg near the light switch, beside the spare car key and the spare house key. I grabbed the office key and the action felt strange. I thought, *I am being strange*. And then I wondered what that meant. If it was my own action how could I judge it? Perhaps it was what my mother would have considered strange. If she had been there she'd have smiled at me and shook her head. "It's too late to be driving to an office to play piano. It's not normal to take something from someone's house unbeknownst to them." *True, mother*, but I took off with the with key anyway.

Inka and I had a habit of renting independent films off the TV at night when we couldn't sleep. We'd probably watched hundreds of them over the five years we'd lived together. In every one there was a scene of a character riding in a car or train, gazing out the window at the floating landscape, brief shots of trees, houses, mountains, flatlands, contemplating their life to an acoustic soundtrack. We would look at each other and laugh when these scenes materialized, so predictably the same. I thought, as I drove into town: Here is mine.

I drove slowly through the snow. It had formed a thin layer on the roads and upon the trees with nothing to disturb it. I watched the sleeping houses and the empty sidewalks. The streetlights changed quickly and I could hear their snap from red to green. I could hear the snow placing itself on the windshield, a graceful splat, and the sounds of the tires and their weight compacting the snow into the road. It was nice to be alone with the sounds. Sounds did not judge and did not try to change you.

In the dark office, the dance room returned to me. The cubicles and computers were shut down and I could see in the shadows formations of little girls, pink tights, hair buns, concentrating their hardest to listen and stand still as Mrs. Malburn circled. They watched her with the same awe as I, as everyone. If she was in a room it was impossible to take your eyes off of her.

Mrs. Malburn was precise in every movement. Opening the door, walking in, arranging the girls in their lines, showing the dance moves, as if her hands were feet: "Frappe one, again, then double." Her posture. Her voice.

Her hair pulled back so smoothly in place. She could never be confused for a "regular person." She was a dancer in every step, word, gesture. Even in the late part of her life, well past a performer's prime, when I knew her. There would be no reason to question or attempt to prove it. To tie her gestures to that of others dancers before, her vocal pattern, her turn out. She was what she was.

By the time I'd reached the piano all the notes were planned. I had the pitches stored, I could see them and hear them: Carlotta's notes and then the shrill and constant peacock sounds. Together they formed a melody. They moved unexpectedly and beautifully. The song formed effortlessly and wholly, so that by the time I reached the end I played the thing through again, verbatim.

It was two in the morning and I called Carlotta on my cell. Another thing my mother would have considered strange. Carlotta's voice was groggy but hopeful on the line.

"Jonis's Lizzy?" she asked.

"I'm sorry it's late but I've written you a song," I told her. "Just now, and I wanted you to hear it. I wanted you to be the *first* to hear it. The song is you. Your pitches that I recorded and the peacock sounds that you gave me. They complement each other perfectly, as if one says what the other can't and together they're complete. Listen..."

I put the phone on top of the piano angled towards its open body so that it peaked at the insides, the naked dinging strings. I played the piece for Carlotta, around ten minutes long, and then I picked the phone up and allowed her some silence.

There was nothing on the line. No sound. But I could feel Carlotta crying.

"Yes," she said finally. "That's exactly how I feel. Can I have it?"

I didn't know in what way she wanted me to give her this song. But in whichever way, it was hers.

"I haven't gotten much more than that. Correlations

of sounds are tricky. I'm really not qualified. I'm no scientist…"

"It was perfect," Carlotta said. "You understand. I want everyone to understand. When I'm with my family and my friends I feel so distant from them. I'm angry at them and they haven't done anything wrong. I can't give them the chance to. I'm glad you called, Lizzy, and I'm glad that *you* know."

"Why don't you tell them?" I asked her.

"I can't have the same conversation with each one of them. It would be so tedious to watch each of their faces turn on me in bewilderment. Daunting."

"I'm sorry," I said. I took time to think of another way, a public announcement? A chain email – but in the end, "I'm sorry I called you so late," was all I could add.

CHAPTER SEVENTEEN

Just before sunrise, Jonis heard a girl shrieking in the hallway. He hobbled out of his room with his hands on the walls for support. He thought first of his mother, of a sound he had heard as a child on the nights before his surgeries. He thought then of me and the way I had mourned the dividing of my family. But when he made it around the corner of his room and down the narrow hall, he found only the grey carpet, the brass framed mirror, the black and white snapshots that hung on the wall of young Jonis standing on two feet.

Jonis considered the Vicodin, but there had been something about the sound, something more than a drug-dream mirage. He felt woozy and leaned his whole weight into the wall. A pain shot from his leg into his back and he hunched forward trapping it. It roamed around his upper ribs and towards his eyes, which scrunched, denting his eyebrows into canopies. He had always been good at breathing, relaxing, releasing, but now he felt too encapsulated by the pain to do anything but hold on to it. He wanted to hold on to it.

There was a liberation to accepting and keeping his pain. In his youth, Jonis had believed that affliction would outcast him. Children have a certain carefreeness, and he feared that to admit the knowledge of sorrow would be to define himself as not a child. Now firmly planted in adulthood, however, pain could be a thing to bind him to the rest. The world was full of misery and defeat. Why should he deny his suffering?

I think of the times in my life when I have been sick: a long flu, a burst appendix, strep throat, etc. There's a gloomy coziness to the memories. Mornings when I woke and decided to go back to sleep because the thought of a day defeated me. The mind plays with pain, turns to it or away. Being sick is an art. Maybe everything is an art, I don't know, but I think that being sick is. Jonis had been working through suffering for years and there, against the wall, came into it.

Cowering, he listened again for the howling and it filled the house. Now not a woman but an animal howling, a cat desperate over the loss of her kittens to a stinky careless truck looping through back roads in search of prey. It groaned and meandered like the ending of a pop song. He searched every room for it, every closet and hall. But there were no animals in his house and no late night singers. The house was empty. The howling faded to a whisper and then it was gone.

Jonis retreated to the bedroom where loneliness arrived like a circus sick of traveling, grudgingly unpacking the ladders and red noses and elephants and all. Jonis stood at the window and watched the snow shiny with morning sun. The flakes formed their Morse codes on the window and he glared at their melting messages so intently that he thought he'd forgotten how to blink until he forced his lids down, reassured. Throughout his life when it snowed or rained Jonis was overcome by the feeling that it would never stop. "I think it will snow forever," he once told me. "I mean, I know it won't but I can't help thinking that it will, it must, the way it comes down so steadily."

The snowdrifts shifted towards his house, piling up

against the siding. He wondered if the wind had ever blown long enough in one direction to pile the snow all the way over the very window he stood before. Perhaps he pictured that episode of *Little House on the Prairie* where the snow covered the Ingalls' house all the way to the roof, and in order to leave they had to tie up a rope from the house to a tree across the way so that they could hold onto it in case they fell in and sank beneath it. Of course, I would have pictured that episode, but I'm not at all sure that Jonis ever watched *Little House on the Prairie* as a child. Either way, he decided he'd keep watching this snow until it made it up to his roof. He decided that if the snow made it, then he'd go back to the way he was before. Unquestioning. Happy. He'd go back to work, to his doctor's appointments, to doting on his girlfriend, and to sleeping through the night without pills. He considered this a reasonable ultimatum with the universe. His depression would no longer be his fault; if he was meant to return to his life then the snow would reach him.

Jonis sat on the floor and partially unwrapped his leg from the pressure bandages that surrounded it. It had been two days since he'd changed them and as his skin hit the air it hurt like a breath out of water after a long stint of breath holding: one Mississippi, two Mississippi, three. He was always winning that game when we played at the gorges the previous summer. His varicose veins looked alien to him, surprisingly deep in their purple rivers. Even the port-wine stain on his calf, which had always been on his calf, seemed larger, skewed. It looked like a dragon, a wild winged beast. He didn't want to see it anymore so he closed the old bandages back around it. The snow was still coming at him, the wind blowing steadily west, and he cracked the window to feel the cold on his face and to distract himself from the smell of his bandages, thick with days' worth of sweat and pus. He knew enough to know he'd been negligent, and perhaps that was his intention. Perhaps it was mine. His gloom had partially coated me as well and when I should have reminded him to change his raps, I grew distracted. When I should have gently cleaned his leg before bed I was busy being angry that he'd taken those pills again and fallen asleep before I even had a chance to say goodnight. The days slung together in such a way that he never realized it was time to re-bandage and neither did I. Such neglect! I can hear the voice of idyllic Nurse Miranda. "I am disappointed." She would run her silky hands on his flesh and massage out the knots. His first love; his first erection. He told me these things as a man will do if properly coaxed and prodded. His leg must have been lonely for her that morning, for her care.

When the phone rang at noon, Jonis was still standing by his bedroom window.

"I've beat the thing," Doug said, full of triumph.

The voice was unexpected and Jonis almost didn't recognize it. They hadn't seen each other since late May, before Doug was diagnosed with hepatitis B. Jonis had called Doug a few times, to hear details of Doug's sickness, to share in it. He should have visited him, but Doug had always been the one to raise Jonis's spirits. Doug forced him out on a Caribbean cruise after a three-week hospital stay the summer after sophomore year, took him bar-hopping every night for two weeks straight after he and Nicollet broke up. Jonis didn't know how to reverse the formula of their friendship. Jonis should have been thrilled now that Doug was better, and their friendship could resume, Doug well and lively and pulling Jonis along. But the news felt unsettling.

"There's this patch of corroded pavement outside my window," Jonis said. "Growing up out of the snow like a triumphant city. The road might be alive."

"Sounds sci-fi!" This excited Doug. Anything about the world would, now that it had been assessed he'd remain in it. "Take a picture! Then you and the picture get the hell over here so we can celebrate my return. I've got beer!" Doug was giddy like a kid, a man with a whole big healthy life ahead.

"To Syracuse?" It was only about 45 minutes but it seemed to Jonis impossibly far away. Any number of things could prevent him from making it. They'd have to. Jonis imagined that any second he and Doug would be disconnected by a fallen phone wire, taken down by the weight of the snow. He imagined a large gust of wind that would shatter the window before him and send him to the ground. He waited, but nothing transpired.

"Pack for the night, bro," Doug said. "I'm not going to let you drive back drunk in this storm."

Doug ran at Jonis and tackled him in the doorway. His crutches flew like extra limbs. When Jonis hit the floor, shoulders first, and watched his leg come crashing down, he realized that he wasn't as fragile as he'd been making himself out to be. He recalled why he had once shrugged off his deformity like a horsefly and in an exciting moment believed that by the sight of Doug alone he had been cured of his depression. *That wasn't so hard. How do these psychologist types make all their money anyway?*

"Where's this pavement castle, show it to me and then throw on something presentable and let's get to the bar," Doug said.

Doug had a green feather in his dark shaggy hair, tied tight at the root. It was a thing he'd been doing for years to make himself more exotic.

Jonis had forgotten about the pavement. He pulled the Polaroid out of his pocket and moved from the doorway into the apartment. He had once lived there with Doug, before Nicollet and well before me. He stood before the bay windows, three evenly shaped sisters looking out from the thirteenth story. He looked at the Polaroid. Before leaving he had walked all the way out to the back patio to get the shot of this strange pavement creature rising up from the ground into the snow. It looked like the road had burst up and was trying to escape. Certainly he'd aimed the camera right at it but in the shot before him, nothing. He scanned the picture and all that was there was white. A picture of snow.

"Aw screw the pavement," he threw the photo on the floor. He slung his arm around Doug. "It's so good to have you back." Though the statement was true, Jonis was aware that he was not being genuine but rather covering up for some strange character flaw that after all they'd been through together – ten years of friendship, five years of living together, those painful two weeks when Doug cared diligently for Jonis because Patty was away and there was a problematic vein swelling and infecting below his ankle – he was suddenly afraid Doug would hate him for this new flaw. And what was this flaw? It wasn't exactly the fact that he had lost his hopeful spirit, it was more a flaw of make-believe, a childish flaw contorting strangely around a man. The howling, the snow city, he couldn't explain them to himself, let alone to Doug. The amputation, his depression, he wondered where he'd be able to hide it all. Before Jonis could decide how little or much to disclose, before he could get a handle on the fact that he'd actually driven up to Syracuse and agreed to go out partying with Doug amidst his beautiful hiatus from all things uplifting, they were already standing outside of the thin neon letters blinking FAT KATHY'S.

It was hard for me to believe at first, but that's actually the name of the place. "Not a nickname you gave it?" I asked Jonis. He assured me it was not a nickname. Kathy took over the bar after her father, BIG JOE, died of cancer. Kathy was an old schoolmate of Patty's, and Patty thought it empowering how she changed the name the way she did, "letting everyone know that you can be a self-assured big woman just like you can be a self-assured big man." Patty never went to bars but her and Kathy would hang out sometimes, part of that same forty-something crew who grew up in upstate New York, circled around it most of their lives, but never left. They went to occasional lunches at the diner when Patty and Jonis lived back in Syracuse and even after Patty's move they continued their annual trip down to the city to see a show on Broadway, always something dark, *Sweeney Todd* or *Phantom*.

Upon entrance, Doug slapped the bouncer high-five. He was a big guy with beautifully crafted mutton chops. The very same bouncer was there when I visited FAT KATHY'S some months later. He was the kind of man who never aged or altered and it seemed always had been and always would be standing there inside the door of the bar. FAT KATHY'S had a brick exterior and no windows to the outside. It was a long narrow hole of a bar that held on to the smell of smoke although it had been years since smoking in bars was legal in the state of New York.

"My first drink in ninety-six days," Doug said, holding up his tequila shot next to Jonis's at the bar. Doug looked at Kathy as he spoke. Doug made a habit of telling her that she was "his type of girl: mysterious, plump, and sexy." She'd cackle crisply, so you could tell she'd never been a smoker, and that she'd never be wooed by a young boy like Doug. Whatever she was looking for, it wasn't him. Or perhaps, like Patty, she'd given up looking.

"Ninety-six long days," Doug repeated.

Kathy's smooth pale skin paunched up around the forehead in response but she didn't say anything.

"Cheers," Jonis said, imagining what kind of man counts the days between drinks: an alcoholic, an obsessive compulsive, a loner, Doug. Isn't it strange how a friendship can escape you, leave you wondering?

Doug pulled his glass away as Jonis went to clink it.

"Too slow!" he said. Jonis didn't laugh.

"Kathy," Doug called, though she was standing right there, "come toast to my recovery!"

Doug held the shot steady. This drink was important,

a return.

"What'cha recovering from?" Kathy asked. "Alcohol-ism?"

Doug winked at Jonis like a lover, a seductress. "Oh life, sickness, heartbreak, all your ruthless rejections… what does it matter, Kathy? I've recovered and that's that." I wonder if Kathy told Patty how Doug flirted with her. I wonder if she reported back to her about the girls Jonis took home after he'd broken up with Nicollet and before he'd met me. Patty had always worried that her son would be unsocial so she urged him to join the world full force, but still, it would be hard to know these things about his adult life. For her to picture him flirting and sloppy, making out with some nameless *chick*, gawking incessantly at his leg. Even for her to imagine him with me, loving me in a way he could never love her. Patty must have wanted, in some ways, for him to remain her brave, deformed, child – the slender jovial figure in and out of hospital beds, telling jokes as his bloody sores were anointed, and only ever crying in the dark.

Kathy poured herself a shot which Doug clinked before and after he clinked Jonis's, and they all drank to his secret ailment, which only Jonis knew the truth of and only Jonis could envy. An ailment like Doug's could be hidden away beneath a secret wink and a leg like Jonis's would always fall into plain sight.

At round six of tequila and approaching ten o'clock, the bar started to fill with the students, a classification which spills away easily once you are no longer one. Kathy got busy mixing up the anatomical shots, fuzzy navels and redheaded sluts. The kids flagged her down with their calm hand movements and their quick eye contact, trying hard to conceal their fake IDs. Jonis felt superior and sad. He wasn't so far out yet, he still knew some of them, having graduated himself only three years before, but they were long years in which the Syracuse campus had come to seem oddly formed like one of those bomb-test neighborhoods: artificial, contained.

There were two girls next to Jonis talking about the nature of Wittgenstein; the taller one argued for perfect language and the other, small with olive pit eyes, for language games. Their arguments were well informed and complex and he imagined they had a class together and had recently been studying modern language philosophy. It was never a good idea to pop into a debate such as this but Doug pulled out the word 'Tractates' and took off.

"The Tractates is suffocating, you can tell right away. A philosophy killer, mind killer, language killer…"

"It is. You're right," the taller girl replied, thin crooked lips that hardly moved as she spoke. She shook his hand and took his name. Doug introduced Jonis and they all nodded and smiled.

Doug and Jonis didn't hang out at "the college bars" anymore, the ones that let you flip a quarter and if you hit heads your drinks were half price. The ones with table dancing contests and the hip DJs. They hung, now, at the townie bars, where people ranged in age rather than clumped around one. Even in college, Jonis had preferred the townie bars, though Doug argued that they'd get better girls at the college bars, and sometimes that was enough to convince Jonis. But he knew that at the college bars, he'd also get those exploitive glances. Those down-shooting eyes from small pretty faces who looked at him and couldn't believe that he could have happened upon the same world as them. The college kids who came to Kathy's made friends with Chain Mail (the middle aged man who came in each night wearing the silver chain-mail that his wife, an apt metalworker, had made for him), they understood how to share a pool table, they didn't wear tank tops in the winter, and when they overdosed on their drugs of choice they were prone to quieter exits, being dragged out the door by a noble friend, not the loud departures of the alcoholic but something harder, more dignified. They came, in part, because they wanted to be surrounded by people drastically different than those they'd bump into on campus. And Jonis was sure different. "Tractates," Doug noted, clearly out of ideas on the subject.

"If Wittgenstein hadn't denounced it, it probably would have killed him," Jonis began. "Imagine being faced with the choice of whether or not to take back your greatest achievement, reject it at its core? I find that more interesting than the theories of language themselves, this choice between the self and the ego."

Doug nodded vigorously.

Jonis thought he might have gotten them, then… "What happened to your leg?" the tall one asked.

No more Wittgenstein. No more philosophy. Her hair was a dark red and before she spoke about his leg, he may have thought her beautiful.

"Got run over by his own motorcycle in a crash," Doug answered for Jonis. "Man, it was a mean sight. Blood and flesh."

The girls winced in a fascinated unison, the response to accidents but never to built-in defects.

"You still ride?" the shorter asked.

The taller shoved her, "Of course he doesn't, stupid."

There was a sisterly way about them which Jonis found endearing. He started to lure them with gory stories of his "accident," the recovery, the strange way a body reforms. He'd always wanted siblings. He suspected that if his mother hadn't first birthed a deformed child, she might have had more through the years, by different men. But how could you live for nine months with the fear? First a boy with a leg much too long, next a girl with a neck that reaches to the sky, a boy with a nose like Pinocchio, a girl with earlobes that twist down to her toes like the old elephant song, "Do Your Ears Hang Low?" She said one was enough and he couldn't blame her.

"I could never ride again. I'm not afraid to admit it," he said boldly. It felt good to lie.

He started planning dates and times, hospital names, doctor's names, he had them all at his disposal anyway. He started planning motorcycle brands, but sadly he could only think of Harley, and he probably didn't look like a Harley guy, or maybe, he wasn't sure, could he pass as a Harley guy?

"Will it ever heal," the short one whispered, to Jonis or to Doug or to no one.

"Yes," Doug said. "We're on our way to recovery!"

Doug reached a fist into the air and it looked so ridiculous up there, his shiny fist hovering above their intellects, waiting to fall down.

"No," Jonis said. "It won't ever heal." Because these girls, he thought, deserved to know.

"Don't be such a downer," Doug said, his green feather fell to the front of his face and the small one reached over and brushed it away from his right eye. "Anyone up for pool?" Doug leaned into the girls conspiratorially. "His crutches are specially made to double as cues!"

"Nuh-uh," the tall one said. "Let me see."

"Just a joke, honey," Doug replied moving to the pool table.

The girl rolled her eyes so meticulously.

"Not a bad idea though. What do ya think, Jon?"

"I think…" He thought that those girls were nothing like him, that Doug looked skinny and good and that maybe sickness agreed with him. He thought that no matter how drunk he got, this routine would be stiff on him. And I'd like to think, he thought about how he missed me. "… nothing. Let's play."

There had been three games of pool. Doug and his olive won two times against Jonis and his girl, but lost the third game to Chain Mail and his wife Lauren who in turn won the table back and took on the next group. Now Doug and Jonis were sitting at a table in the corner. The small girl, with olive-branch skin and green pit eyes, had her hand on Doug's shoulder when Doug whispered in Jonis's ear that he was "*so* horny." Jonis poked his shoulder hard, twice, with sporty aggression. "Clean slate," Doug said to the group, motioning with both hands. "We need to clear this all up and get us another round."

His arms flailed and he started off on his squeaky reed laugh, which continued on until the waitress cleared the drinks and appetizers they had ordered and brought back some fresh Jaeger bombs – pound, pound, and drink.

Their fists shook the table together and the Jaeger dropped into the beer with a thud. It should have been nice for Jonis, hanging with his best friend in a young and social city, but he hated the way his dark denim felt around his waist and more how they looked over his leg, cutting off mid-way through his elongated shin and leaving a foot long gap of leg before his sling started with its monstrous black bag attached. His shoe, on the left foot where he wore one, was tight around the sides, either it was constricting or he was expanding and he hated to spend money on a whole new pair when he could only wear the one. Doug's glass took off onto the floor and the taller girl picked it up.

"Oh, that's it," Doug said while she was on the ground retrieving it. "She looks like Nicollet, right? I knew it was someone. I've been trying to figure it out all night."

And in a way, Jonis thought, she did. She was lanky and sharp. She had that smattering of freckles under her eyes.

Doug wiped some beer off his face with his fist and pecked at his olive with quick kisses. He giggled something at her and grabbed the in-curve of her waist. "Let's take this party back to my place," he said to all of them, but only to her.

Doug winked at Jonis. Doug had met me only twice and he couldn't quite get a handle on the fact that Jonis wasn't single anymore. Doug couldn't get a handle on the fact that he may have been better but he still wasn't entirely cured. He would take that girl home. He would contaminate her.

"I think we should steer clear of your house at all costs," Jonis said. He couldn't let it happen. "Because of the person residing there."

Doug wasn't yet baffled. He was waiting for the punch line.

"Who's residing there?" Doug asked. "The boogey man?"

"Your wife."

They all looked at Doug accusingly.

"He's kidding."

"Maybe I am, maybe I'm not."

"Fuck off, Jon."

Doug stood up to walk away, cool down. Jonis picked up a crutch and swung it at Doug, "playfully" harder than he'd expected to. He got him in the back of the knees and took him down like a gangster. It felt nice when Doug fell but Jonis was afraid when Doug stood up again.

Doug pulled him by the shirt and dragged him away from the table as Jonis crutched haphazardly to keep up.

"What are you doing, Jon?"

"What are *you* doing? How could you even think of it…"

"I'd wear a condom. Calm down… What the hell? There really is something wrong with you. Who's to say I'd get laid anyway? I'm just having a good time. You expect me to never date again for the rest of my life? I was fucking sick … nice of you to visit … nice of you to care."

"This *is* me caring."

"This is you jealous because I'm having fun. I'm

getting better and you're not, because you've forgotten how, because you're in some kind of dark hole and your little girlfriend is letting you sit there and rot and you're both too self-absorbed to see out of it."

"You're fucked," Jonis screamed as loud as he could.

Jonis went to hit him with his crutch again but Doug caught it and pulled Jonis to him. Doug gave him this look where his cheeks frame the rest of his face like an apology, then punched him once, hard in the eye. Doug helped Jonis catch his balance before walking away.

"That's all you got?" Jonis called after him with a sadistic laugh.

"No," Doug said. "Take this, too." Doug threw his apartment keys. They hit Jonis in the stomach where they bounced away and fell to the floor. "Grow the fuck up."

Jonis stood still for a moment and watched the eyes of people staring and then slowly, sadly, turning away. He groveled to pick up the keys and Kathy approached him.

"I'm fine," Jonis said.

She nodded. It was unclear how much or little she had seen of the "fight."

"Your mother worries you're losing touch," she said.

"What the fuck? Did she call ahead, Kathy?"

Kathy looked to the floor. Jonis put his hand on Kathy's shoulder.

"Don't worry about me," he said.

"Come visit us more often. Doug misses you."

"Yeah..." Jonis pointed to his eye.

"I miss you. I like watching you crutching around, catching all the girls' eyes. You know, Nicollet was in asking..."

"She has no right to ask anything."

"She wanted to know you were all right. I told her all about your new girl. I thought that's what you'd have wanted me to do. I'd love to meet her, you know, your knew girl. Bring her by...your mom tells me she's a gem."

"Is that what she tells you?"

"Yeah, she does. Direct quote. I was surprised, too. Wait here."

Kathy rummaged behind the bar for a moment and emerged with a bag of ice that she placed in Jonis's hand, and then on his eye. "Get back safe now," she said.

Jonis was sprawled on the living room carpet watching the snow when Doug started banging on the door. Jonis thought of hiding, the closet or the bathtub. Under the bed? Inside the cupboard?

After a few minutes of banging Doug gave up, he went to his mailbox in the lobby, entered his pass code and took out his spare key. He let himself into his apartment and took a seat next to Jonis on the floor. They watched the snow together for a while.

"Feels like old times," Doug said. "Before couches."

"You remember that party we had during the black out when the elevators were down?" Jonis replied.

"And I had to climb down and up thirteen flights of stairs to make a beer run," Doug said.

"Better you than me!" Jonis touched the floor beside him where the carpet had gone wet from the melting bag of ice he'd placed there. "I had dream about that night. It's one of those dreams that you swear you've had a few times but aren't quite sure. It's one scene: you and I and some other people who vary are sitting on the floor playing quarters, we throw down and then everything goes black and all the quarters hit the floor at the same time and the house shakes and you reach out to grab me and I see your arm in the dark before I fall through the floor."

"What does it mean?" Doug asked.

"I'm guilty, for not visiting you."

"Guilty as charged."

Doug looked at Jonis, one of those serious tell-me-your-problems-for-real glares. "Jonis, you look like mold and sort of smell like it, too. Are you growing mold?"

Jonis laughed and the laughing hurt his eye; he winced. He could feel it swelling.

"Let me see." Doug turned Jonis's head and poked at his puffy cheek.

Doug looked at his hands after having touched Jonis, got up, and went into the bathroom.

"Shit, I'm not that gross," Jonis called as he heard Doug turn on the water.

"I know, but your leg, man. I think your leg might be," he said upon return.

He was right.

Doug unwrapped Jonis's bandages carefully. He took a warm soapy wash cloth and wiped down Jonis's leg. He put peroxide on the swollen spots, rubbed some Neosporin in. Doug had seen Jonis repeat his ritual of cleaning and wrapping hundreds of times in the years they had lived together.

"That smells better."

"It's not like I haven't been showering," Jonis said.

"Hey, bro, I know. It's not easy. Being sick, or whatever, I know it's not easy... You got any more raps? I'm not putting those old things back on."

"There's some in the car. But don't worry about it. I'll get them in the morning. The air will be good for it for tonight."

Doug got Jonis a blanket and pillow and some more ice for his eye.

"Goodnight, Jon."

"Hey, Doug, where's your girl?"

"Maybe I did her in the taxi on my way home."

"Hey, Doug..."

"Yes?"

"Thanks."

Jonis lay back on the carpet and rested the ice on his face. In the distance he thought he could hear the howling. It sounded like a man this time, cold and sad and alone. The ice fell to the carpet and formed a pillow-puddle under his head as he drifted to sleep. He imagined it as snow crawling in through the thirteenth-story window and surrounding him. It numbed him. The howling grew faint and faded further and further away until it disappeared and the room was silent except for the pulse of his breath and his own occasional snore.

CHAPTER EIGHTTEEN

Jonis came to my apartment in the late afternoon in spirits much different then they'd been the night before. For his opening gesture, he took his bottle of Vicodin out of his pocket and threw it to me across the room. I held the bottle gently like a fish with spikes. It was such a small cylindrical object and yet so powerful.

"Keep 'em," he said. "I'm finished with my moping."

I gave Jonis a kiss, threw the bottle into the kitchen junk drawer, and hastily cooked up some grilled ham and cheese sandwiches.

"A slice of tomato on mine?" he requested. But I couldn't remember if the tomatoes that sat on the counter were Inka's or mine. Had I used my last tomato in the salad last night or had there been one more?

"No," I whispered.

"There's one right there…"

"No."

I felt uncomfortable being with him inside my apartment. I kept an eye over my shoulder as the bread browned in the pan to see that Inka hadn't come out of her room to scowl at us. When Jonis spoke I feared his voice was too loud, that it might summon her. I found myself whispering, tiptoeing, wiping off the stove and countertops once and then again to be sure there was no trace of us, nothing for Inka to lodge a complaint about.

"I have an idea," Jonis said once we'd finished eating our sandwiches, and pulled me out the door.

We escaped to Jonis's where there was nothing to fear. The door swung easily open to the dark house of cinnamon (Patty) and aquatic cologne (Jonis). I hung my jacket on the coat rack and the silence confirmed that Patty was out for the night.

"Your idea?" I asked.

"I want to measure it," Jonis said and then rushed into his bedroom.

"Why?" I called down the hall after him to no response.

I watched Jonis's leg take on a warm hue as he spread it out on the bed. His compression bandages unraveled on the blankets like intestines. I unbuttoned his jeans to find his slender waist inside. It was the kind of waist I had possessed as a girl, tight skin and bone, and sometimes when I felt around my middle now soft and curved, I missed being so contained. I unzipped his jeans down each side and tossed them off the bed. His leg seemed so tender that I wanted to kiss it. I began below his toes and kissed my lips upon his leg all the way to the top. I kissed over clammy skin, over thick red rashes, over fresh gauze bandages and deep purple veins. One hundred and twenty three kisses. Jonis closed his eyes and placed his hands lightly together as if he were praying; he may have been. "The tape measure," he said, and pointed to the end table. I ran the cool plastic down from his knee to his foot. Thirty-three inches until the bone stopped, sixty more until the very bottom of his foot, the large, thick, big toe.

"Ninety-three and a half," I said.

Jonis nodded and repeated the number in a soft push of air, "Ninety-three and a half inches. As long as it gets.

"You've made it stop growing," he said. "I've always

been able to feel the growth, you know, like you can feel swelling in your eyes when you cry or after an injury."

"Like this here?" I reached towards his eye, which was inexplicably puffy and blue around the cheekbone.

"Don't touch," he swatted me gently away. "We'll get to that story later. I want to talk about my leg," he said. "It's been months now since I've felt anything. It's stopped. It's still. It's reached the end."

I moved towards Jonis's head and nudged against his body in a small cocoon. I thought of an image Inka had instilled in my mind before I'd slept with Jonis of a long, deformed extremity running between his legs, "A dick to match his leg," she said and I did my best to push it away.

I thought of our first time. It had been a warm night, the windows open, the breeze coming in. I had tried so hard to focus on Jonis's face but I couldn't keep myself from finding a strange creature in the bed along with us. It had seemed impossible then that I'd ever be able to make love to him without thinking of his leg, worrying where it was and if I might hurt it. I'd watched a documentary once on a pair of conjoined twins who were both dating different men. They'd affixed a thick velvet curtain in the middle of the bed so that they could be 'alone' with their lovers. And I thought of them, on that warm summer night. I had driven over late after he was already in bed, and his leg was unwrapped and strewn out before me. I just wanted to be alone with Jonis, but his leg was there too. I sat down on Jonis's bed in the only spot I could find, up near his chest. Jonis grabbed for his bag from the floor, to contain his leg so that it wasn't in the way. "I'll get it," I said. I reached over the bed and slid the back towards me and as I sat back up and pulled the bag onto the bed, I bumped into his foot, causing it to slip off the side of the bed and land on the wooden floor, pulling some of his leg along with it – an odd deranged Slinky. I picked up Jonis's foot and placed it at the foot of the bed. "I'm sorry," I said to it earnestly. There was a bloody taste in my mouth, and when Jonis came to kiss me I pulled away, not wanting him to know this taste of rust and fear. But he tried again and again until I stopped resisting. The taste, if it had ever been there at all, disappeared.

Now, I looked out the window; it had started snowing again. Jonis sat up and grabbed his bag off the floor as he had done so many times, but tonight I didn't want any part of him hidden.

"No," I said. "Keep your leg out so I can see it."

Jonis grabbed behind my neck with one hand and pushed the duffel to the floor with the other and it landed haphazardly as his foot once had. I closed my eyes and the world softened.

There was the illusion of creation as we kissed. I was composing, strong chords and elegant runs. I could hear his tongue circling mine in soft piano notes that grew louder when he bit my lower lip and softer as he moved his fingers under my bra and held the weight of my breast in his hand. It was a simple rhythm, dissonant harmonies, and a melody I could almost hum. I wanted to run to a piano and play before this masterpiece escaped, but I needed him too strongly to leave time for notation.

I kissed my lips down his torso and felt the muscles of his stomach contract. I reached into his boxers, moving down along the bed, hunched and groveling. I pushed him into my soft upper pallet. Cupped in my warmth I wanted to keep him there where he couldn't be harmed. He filled me just short of suffocating and then pulled my upper body towards him with a strength that alarmed me. We were rocking back and forth and I could hear the oscill-ation of our harmonies, not in metaphor but in reality as if there were actually a pair of methodical hands pounding ivory keys right there in his bedroom. I thought of the musical hallucination that Petey had explained, and despite all the music I had heard and played in my life, I, like Petey, had never heard music like this before.

When we finished I closed my eyes and tried to focus

on the melodies that I, or we, had made; but they were elusive. All I could hear was his breathing and my breathing. I felt tears rushing like insulted armies towards my eyes. I felt loss.

"Why are you crying?" he asked me.

"It was a beautiful song," I said. And I thought for certain that I would have loved him still if his penis hadn't ended up being perfectly normal.

You should write more," he said, trying, as he did sometimes, to figure me out. "You hear the music everywhere, in places no one else does."

"I wrote a song for Carlotta. I'll play it for you at the office next time."

Jonis sat up abruptly. "We can move the piano here," he said. "I don't know why I didn't think of it before."

"Will your mother mind?" I asked.

"Why should she mind? She loves it when you come to the office and play. We have plenty of space."

I settled back into Jonis's arms and pictured myself playing in a lovely living room instead of a cramped office.

"Finally, Mrs. Malburn's piano will have a real home," I said. "You know, I haven't felt 'home' since I moved away for college. I was wandering, but not anymore."

Jonis kissed me and I heard the echoes of our song.

"I have to tell you something," Jonis said. "I've finally figured it out, the whole fear of pride thing, the reason that the Dahlia Lama can live the way he does. I've figured out what lies behind everything he says. It's detachment. It's so simple. Releasing, letting go. He tries to explain it in a hundred different ways, but still, I didn't really understand. And now I do. See, if you don't hold on to ideas of what you are, who you are, ideas of things like home, then you'll always be who you are and what you are; wherever you are will be home. It's the holding on that betrays you, causes anger and grief and unhappiness."

"You sound very Buddhist."

"You're not listening, Lizzy. I'm not anything, or

rather, I just want to be me. I'm going to have the amputation. I'm going to let go."

When my cell phone began to ring it hardly interrupted the ringing of his phrase, 'I'm going to have the amputation. I'm going to let go.' It was a quiet beeping. It was part of a dream. It was nothing I couldn't ignore amidst my grief, my fear, and my exuberance. Someday Jonis might fit through doorways, walk on two legs; he would be free. But the phone rang again, and then again, persisting until I was forced to answer. Inka's voice on the line was interspersed with weeping. I went to her.

CHAPTER NINETEEN

Inka sat folded into a pike on her bed, wrapped in a fuzzy throw. Her legs seemed too short. Stumpy partial limbs that could hardly hold the long ribcage and head looming above them. As Inka cried, her torso bobbed in the slice of light cutting in from the street lamps. Her computer played sad songs in the boring flat tones of emo boy bands.

I said "honey" as I walked into the room: it was what my mother would have said. I held her.

Inka never had a mother who would hold her; I had been lucky. Had been. In the past months the thought of going to my mother had become terrifying. Everything was changing and I hadn't yet arrived at the new meaning. Mommy – the signifier sounded the same but nothing was similar about what it signified. "Mommy, Mommy." I'd chanted that name so many times when the world was hard or unfair, and now the chant had turned from a plea for help to a plea for dissolution.

"How did it happen?" I asked. My feet were freezing from the drive over. I pulled away from Inka and took a more comfortable position at the end of her bed, covering my feet with her comforter. I was glad that the lights weren't bright enough to require direct eye contact between us.

"We went out last night for our six-month anniversary. He was quiet for the whole first part of dinner, and I couldn't stop thinking that I had totally pushed him away. Last week he told me that his lease was up in his apartment, and he was wondering if we might try living together. He made it sound so pleasant: we'd split the rent and he has all this new furniture. He'd pay the cable bill and cook me dinner at night. It could have worked out, but when he suggested it I started crying. It was too soon for something like that. I've never lived with anyone but you. What would my mom think? And you know how I hate having to share my bed."

I nodded. She did hate to share her bed.

"I think he really loved me, Lizzy," Inka began and then tumbled into a series of cacophonous sobs.

This was hardly the kind of story I had expected to hear, but then Inka never told a story in which she was the undesirable party.

"Once he started talking at dinner, I wished he hadn't. He told me that I wasn't ready to be where he was," Inka said, moving closer to me like a puppy yearning for warmth at the foot of the heater on a February night. "And he might be right, I can't argue with that. But then he said he's interested in this bitch at work. Bonnie. I bet she has big fucking puking breasts that reach right up over her face. Bonnie started dating someone recently, and Carl wants to explain his feelings to her before she gets too serious with this other guy, before he loses his chance. 'She's one of the top law students in the department,' he said, and I could hear loud and clear how stupid he thinks I am. He gave me an ultimatum. Either I had to tell him that I was committed or he was going to HAVE to pursue Bonnie."

"What an asshole!" I was momentarily convinced.

"I know. How did I get stuck with someone like that? I finally decided to open myself up and look, just look…"

I watched the black and white picture show that Inka

was. She called out her pains and his faults. She accepted
no blame. She tossed swear words around the room, and
they bounced politely against the dusty furniture. I wondered how I could help her. I wanted to. What would she
have done had the situation been reversed: told me to suck
it up, told me about how hard her life was to make me feel
better? No, I wouldn't have called her if Jonis had left me,
that was the truth. Who would I call? Not Inka. Not my
mom. My father would have no idea what to say; I would
end up consoling him. The scenario couldn't work. There
was no one to go to but Jonis. There was nothing but
Jonis. He was the only one who knew me anymore.

I started to cry. But it wasn't for my new loneliness,
and it certainly wasn't for Inka. I was crying because I was
fed up, tired, cold. I wanted to go home, which meant
back to Jonis and his bed, back to my life. I wanted my
freedom from Inka. I wanted an ending where an ending
was due. I was the lover who had waited around for way
too long. I was my mother. I had no pity left. And Inka,
poor Inka, expected nothing of me that a friend shouldn't
have been able to provide.

"Did you think you loved him?" I asked softly.

"Don't be snide," she sniffled. "Do you think I've
gone and changed everything I believe in over one boy?
Some of us aren't that easily unwound."

I wondered what I had ever seen in Inka. Isn't that
always the question?

"He wasn't good enough," I offered. "That's why you
didn't love him. He didn't like your family."

"He was rich and smart … and *I* don't even like my
family."

I tried a different tactic: "I know you'll get through
this. You'll find someone who would never think of asking
out anyone else when they are with you, or even when they
aren't."

Inka nodded in acceptance. I didn't believe that there
really was anyone like this out there for her, or for anyone.

A true singular love. All people have versatile needs, shifting feelings, hearts that can wander from one love to another if given the opportunity. And if there was someone, a person that wanted only one thing, then it wasn't due to love but to some other obsession. Singularity might be an illness, a sick closure from which a sufferer, for whatever reason, cannot escape. I didn't hope for a singular love or life for myself. But I knew that Inka did.

"We all hope for different things, I guess," I said to Inka as some kind of comfort.

"And even when we get what we hoped for, we end up miserable," Inka replied. I nodded in a sad agreement.

The moonlight was draining slowly, covered by clouds, and Inka was a thin ghostly shadow now. I feared that a gust might come through our window and blow her away. I hoped it would come.

"You want me to put on some tea? It'll make you feel better," I asked.

I headed to the kitchen and flicked on the lights, buzzing fluorescent yellow. I was tired of dirty kitchens in cheap apartments. I watched the charred pot as it lit with flames, warmed, and finally began screaming. Inka hated that scream but I wanted to hear it, if only for a moment. That enchanting E, airy and sharp as not even the most overzealous soprano could be.

"A mild chamomile, lightly sweetened," I mocked a tea connoisseur as she often mocked those of wine, "buttery and sweet," and I handed her the steaming mug.

The time was nearing 3 AM. I watched the clock, 2:51, 2:57, 2:59, and sipped at my own cup of tea. I felt my nose and throat soften with the steam. I picked at my fingers until there were skin tears across my thumb. I rubbed the scattered skin against my top lip, feeling its brittle resistance. Soon I would reach that soft pink underbelly which gave way to blood. 3:01, 3:03, 3:07. Inka's mug sat firmly on her desk and she began to sulk down into her pillows.

"You don't have to stay, Lizzy," she told me, a temptress and a liar.

Jonis and I had stopped sleeping at my apartment weeks ago when Inka started refusing to dine with us or even to say hi when passing in the common spaces. I had basically taken to living over at Jonis's and stopping in at my and Inka's place occasionally to refresh supplies of clothes and the likes.

"I'm going to sleep," Inka declared. "You can go back to him. I'm fine."

I took her teacup and my own into the kitchen and placed them in the sink. I offered an awkward sideways hug and the promise that tomorrow we would get dinner and some drinks after work. I had no illusion that I was doing the right thing, or that she might forgive me for leaving her when she so desperately didn't want to be alone. But I no longer belonged here. I no longer belonged to Inka. I didn't want to spend the night in that cough syrup room with the shadowy ghost of a girl I had once loved.

I rested my hand on the doorknob, a moment of choice. What similar choices had others that I loved made? A time when my father could have taken his wife's hand but he did not. When my mother could have confided in her husband the stories of her day, but she chose rather to spare herself the effort, to tell them to Jane, the one who she knew desired them more. I turned the knob with the thought that we give each other up too easily, and for that, I was sorry.

And so I returned to Jonis's kisses, his little symphonies with their perfectly timed beats and rhythms, the space between each kiss as important as a rest in a grand concerto.

"Oh silent anticipation," Jonis said, his face hovering above mine.

"Shh, no words."

He pushed his forehead into mine, a soft crescendo, and then our lips touched again so that I could escape back into our song. I could picture the staff as it flooded with notes, and what beautiful, beautiful notes, which I could never recall once our lovemaking ended and we rolled away to our separate sides of the bed.

These kisses, too, would be lost. I would having nothing to prove that I needed to return to him on that night, nothing that I could wave before Inka's face while calling, "See, this is real. My love for him is real. Here it is: this is what it created, this haunting melody!" Nothing that would let her know she was wrong not to forgive me for loving another, wrong to make me let her go. We are not all meant to be Buddhas.

CHAPTER TWENTY

Dear Lizzy or Dearest,

When I first laid eyes on you, you were neat in that way of new shoes. I prefer worn. You stood in my doorway with the smile of a pleaser and though my son had no idea, for I could always read him then, I could tell that you already loved him.

It was a comfort to me that you fell for him so quickly; I didn't know that it would be. I am the jealous type. Jonis's father contacted me once when Jonis was thirteen. Jonis doesn't know this. He will never know this. This man, not a father, I will call him N, found out about my boy, narcissistically assumed that it must have been his, not allowing that I could have been sleeping with anyone else that summer of 1987 when the rain was so persistent. He happened to be right. N contacted me through a letter. The note was simple. He didn't ask to see this son, or inquire as to what he was like. He only let me know that he knew what I had kept from him. I read the note a thousand times and couldn't decide if it was a gesture of confession or a threat — trying to prove that he was the one in charge after all, which was something N would do. I never answered him. I never looked up his address. I never called the number printed at the bottom in his large sloppy numbers as if he'd never grown up. But I worried for months after, for years after, that N would get lonely one night and come for my boy. I never questioned where Jonis's loyalty would lie, I have always known his love, but even one smile from Jonis to the stranger, even one thought of what it might have been like to be raised by this man instead of me. I couldn't bear it!

But with you in my living room on that first evening, it was different. "My," I thought to myself, "aren't you good, Patty? Aren't you just a good person?" Motherhood can do that — surprise you about the thing you thought you knew best, yourself. I didn't think for one moment of rejecting you. I didn't begrudge that you'd take him away from me, as surely you would. I only offered out my handshake and a glass of lemonade. I thought of this letter which I might someday compose to you and in fact now am, explaining this turn in my person. I thought of holding you one night beside my son's grave, sharing the loss with the only other woman who could know it, and feeling almost like him, with you in my arms.

Patty

Jonis was at lunch with a potential client, Patty was in London set to return that afternoon, and I was snooping in Patty's fishbowl. My intention was not to snoop through Patty's belongings but to talk with her when she returned from home from her trip that had something to do with tampons — a new brand that used a soft pull loop instead of a string to avoid the ever awkward situation of a tampon string hanging out from one's underwear or bathing suit without one's knowledge. It seemed like a good idea to me. I hoped that she'd return having gained the account so that she would be in an amiable mood.

I wanted to sit down on her couch and explain to her how frightened I was for Jonis. I would beg her to tell me every last thing that amputation would entail. I wanted to cry. Crying was something I put into my plan. I wanted to cry in order to gain Patty's sympathy so that she would know how much I loved her son, and even so that she might love me.

But then I found the letter in her fishbowl.

After reading the letter, everything about my plan felt

cockamamie. There was a larger issue, which I had not made myself name until I read over that final image in Patty's letter for the third time. The issue was that of Life and Death. By influencing Jonis's amputation decision, I was changing the course of his life. He would *live* in a different way. He would *die* in a different way.

I sat down on Patty's bed. A tightly-made bed with a plain blue comforter, not a wrinkle or crease. The bed was intimate, a place where Patty slept, dreamt, and what else? In all the time that I had been with Jonis there was never mention of a lover. Jonis and I had been spending so much time together and what did she do? She traveled for business ventures, never pleasure. She worked late at the office. She talked on the phone at night to her old college friends, but she rarely went to visit them. She must have been lonely, but she never did seem that way. Jonis was her life.

I recalled Jane's old refrain: "You're her life now," she'd say. But in *my* mother's case, that may never have been true. My mother had a secret existence that had nothing to do with me. In a way, this was a relief. I had seen my mother as a sort of partial person, who popped right out of existence when I wasn't around to draw her to life. I had felt this as a burden, and now, I could see that it was also a terribly naive misconception. How long had they been lovers, she and Jane? It was possible that for as long as I'd been in this world she'd been leading a double life. Jane hadn't been entirely wrong, her lies *had* been for me. Otherwise she would probably have left my father at the time she stopped loving him. Children get in the way of cause and effect.

Still, I hadn't realized that my mother's love for me could be measured. I'd maintained the childish idea that my parents really did love me more than anyone else's parents loved them for years too long and now in Patty's bedroom the whole intact sand dollar of it was finally shattering. I could feel in Patty a different kind of love, a love far exceeding the one my parents ever needed to have for me. Patty had for Jonis a beautiful, heartbreaking, and all-encompassing devotion. He was her grand creation in this world. My own love for him, no matter how intense, could never compare. This was okay; I could live with it. But there was another piece that jolted me. That despite Patty's love for Jonis being stronger and truer, he could still love me more. He would amputate his leg because he loved me. Because he wanted the chance at a life where he was not the ever-patient being cared for, he wanted a chance at a different kind of love.

I sprawled out across Patty's bed and stared up at the ceiling, the air around me surged with the weight of it all.

I could see a future where Jonis would die old, on a Wednesday. I would be there to hold him at the moment of his departure, to hear the pitch of his last sound, *A natural*, fading out to silence. He'd have been pale that winter, translucent. He'd be composing an article on the collapsible ironing board, an invention tied oddly to his own history – a great, great uncle of his was the inventor. "It will be a reflective piece," he'd say to me over tea in the newly renovated sunroom, "about the impact of a life." He would still complain of missing his leg, even so many years after it was taken. Sometimes he would feel the illusion of weight; other times he would experience the striking absence.

He would take to cigars late in life and in the evening. He would learn the clarinet and practice diligently as only adults can, so that eventually he could play with me, lovely duets that would make him cheer or cry at their completion. His teacher, a girl I knew from college, would say he was her favorite student, and she'd come every few weeks for dinner and to join in our ensemble afterwards. Sometimes our daughter would join us too. She would sing.

Jonis would bring flowers to his daughter's home on

Sundays, creative bouquets in varying colors and sizes. From time to time I'd make myself a list of the small alterations and achievements that Jonis had won – his first time in a paddle boat, in a yoga class, dancing at our pretend daughter's wedding – and hold them up as justifications, things that couldn't have been done if he hadn't removed his leg. This was the version of the story that I attached myself to, I could feel it, and I so wanted to believe it. But like a contorted reel, there were other versions of this story playing at the same time.

A hospital's call, "… your husband … pulmonary embolism…" I could feel the distinct shadow of this other death, *his* other death. The death from a world where I, Lizzy, the girl Jonis loved, would not, could not, let him sacrifice a piece of himself. A world where he died not of old-age complications at 75 but of something else, something quicker, a blood clot, a lung complication due to infection at 43, 39? Maybe I would be among friends when the call came in, friends that I would always regret having known since they would keep me, in this moment, from him. Maybe in this death, Patty would be there by this side, as she'd always expected to be. And maybe this was right. How I could rob her of this conclusion?

But there was still another possibility that I refused to consider. At the time, that very afternoon in the bedroom (while I stared up at the ceiling and wondered why it was that ceilings always had such strange and uneven textures, oblong bumps and ridges like those on Jonis's long leg, intricate enough to be stared at forever), I just could not see it. Modern medicine holds such promise. That Jonis would be dead within thirty days of his amputation is something I couldn't have conceived of, for death looming years away is something we can live with, but when it's close by, breathing on your neck in the night, planting sweet new lover kisses on your closed eyes, ticking down a clock you didn't know existed, or maybe you knew, but you thought this clock was set to last so much longer.

This death was impossible for me to believe in.

Patty found me on her bed, curled and wet from sobbing, though the sobs were through by that time. Despite my planning I had not been able to save them for her.

"You're interesting today," Patty said.

I shot up to my feet and wiped at my face. The letter was sitting by my side, unfolded.

Patty sat down on the bed and motioned for me to sit again, beside her.

"The letter…" I said.

"It's all right. I might have given it to you someday."

"Thank you," I said. "I love it."

"It's a thing I do. It lets me say things I might never say, the things that need to be said, and then if I get guts I have the thoughts there to give. Usually the point of honesty and the point of bravery don't match up."

I pulled my legs up onto the bed and hugged my knees.

"I started it a long time ago, when I first found out Jonis was sick. There's letters for him, letters for lost lovers, and many for my mother, who's been dead for most of my life."

"Does Jonis write letters?"

"I don't know. I've never received one. Have you?"

I shook my head. "I have no love letters," I said. "My last boyfriend moved to the city and I waited and waited for a letter from him but all I got were two-line emails."

"Emails never do," Patty said. She folded up her letter and handed it to me. "You keep this one."

I wished I had something equally as meaningful to hand to her. It would be nice to have letters saved up to hand out when you felt you needed to show a person how much you cared, how much you needed them. I thought of Carlotta and what the letter might allow her. It was not impersonal like an email, or formal like an announcement, but it would not be as hard as meeting each relation face to face. She could send letters to all the important people in her life, explaining her past life, her visions, her beliefs. She could explain it all out and then when she saw them again they would know. She could invite them all over and feel free. She could have a party. A party for all to come and talk to her and support her. A coming out! I was excited and almost burst the whole strange story out to Patty, but I saw she had taken on a serious air.

"Perhaps they'll publish them someday: *The Letters of Patricia Stark*," she said.

I hadn't heard her call herself by her full name before. She tilted her head up and smiled mockingly. She looked as sure as royalty that she'd be remembered. I had no such hopes. I knew that no one save a few relatives would think of me after I died; a husband, a child, a close friend, and that was all right by me. As long as there were those few. This was such a small and pleasant thought that it filled the whole room. I felt warm and safe…and maybe happy?

I reached out and hugged Patty. I could feel by her tightness that it was unexpected. I wanted to tell her all about my fears for Jonis as I had planned to. Further, I wanted to tell her that he had decided on amputation and that it was all my fault and that I was sorry that he was going against what she thought was right. I wanted acceptance for him and forgiveness for me. Of course I couldn't tell her any of this. It wasn't my place. I hoped that Jonis did take after his mother and write letters and I hoped that he had one ready to hand to her before things proceeded on much further. I kept holding tight to Patty and I felt so near to her. *Tell her something*, I thought, *to let her know that you trust her.* "My mother's having an affair with a woman," I said and then I released Patty so that I could catch her expression. She looked calm and I was disappointed. I had wanted a response closer to what I was feeling: complete astonishment at having admitted this fact out loud for the first time and for no reason other than my personal gain.

"Does your father know?"

"Yes."

"Love has so many consequences." Patty patted my hands, still clasped tight around my knees. She took the time to gain my eye contact and to hold it. "Let her go a bit," Patty said. "You have to."

CHAPTER TWENTY-ONE

I was a dashing peahen, a Java Green. An array of browns, golds, whites, and creams crested up my back and peaked at the top with a brown and white spotted feather I had ravaged every craft store in the area to find. I was adorned with a fluffy white mask across my nose and up onto the top of my head where seven small feathers sprouted straight up, adding, as I had often hoped my late onset puberty would, at least two inches to my height. My eyes were painted with eyeliner and shadowed white all around to make them as wide as any female bird in her prime. Though it was Jonis, going as an India Blue cock, who was able to wear that brilliant tropical blue, I still felt beautiful, transformed as I had been on the Halloweens of childhood when I had indulged in just the right fantasy.

Carlotta called it "a coming out party," borrowing the phrase from me. There was first a letter, long and exposing, and then this invitation: "Friends, in support of my new lifestyle, please join me by dressing up as a peacock for my coming out party. Be elaborate! Be unafraid. Invite as many guests as you can find. Ask me anything you want about what it's like to have lived a past life!" I was so proud of Carlotta that I hung the invitation on the refrigerator. This is how it happened that Inka got a look at it.

"Oh, you're kidding me," Inka said. She began squawking around the kitchen. It was good to see Inka up and moving. She'd been sulking in her room for the past three weeks. I'd checked on her a few times, brought her dinner once because I was afraid she would starve herself in there, but other than that there had been little contact between us. We passed each other in the apartment silently. Some nights Inka would dress hastily, after having made arrangements on the phone with whom I suspected to be new friends or a new boyfriend. She usually didn't return until the next day and sometimes she spent the whole weekend away. She never invited me.

"I'm totally coming," Inka declared. "You know I love to dress up!"

I recalled what I loved about Inka, her energy. The apartment felt alive again with our forgotten chatter and laughter, a soundtrack of our friendship that had lately been turned down so low it was inaudible.

"Jonis is coming," I noted cautiously.

"I assumed."

"And his mother, I think. You'll like Carlotta, though. She's very intuitive."

"Maybe I'll pick me up a hot bird!" Inka laughed and took off to her room to Google sexy peacock costumes. She called me in every few minutes to preview. "This one comes with a head piece... That one's attached to a leotard... Could you even fit through a doorway in that one?" As I peered over her shoulder at the numerous images of peacock attire, I thought we might be mending, she and I.

And so, on the night of the party, after a preliminary shot of Grey Goose at my apartment, Jonis, Patty, Inka and I, passed as a flock from house, to car, through many long stop lights, and held our heads high as pioneers of our kind, flaunting feathers and calling out the cry of caution, fear, and excitement: "Woo woo woo woo!"

Carlotta had rented out a banquet hall downtown. The hall was decorated with feathers of every sort. They hung on the walls and from the ceiling creating an exotic new land. Jonis waddled sideways through the door and I had to look away from him in order not to burst out in laughter. Never had a man looked stranger. His face and neck were painted entirely blue save for his yellow nose, his feathers spread out in a five foot radius, his leg protruded behind him with its usual duffel, and he could hardly move himself along on his crutches without running into something or someone, feathers bumping and his polite "excuse me's." He was poignantly non-human.

There was quite a turnout; at least forty people filled the room, flaunting tails and wagging beaks. I found Carlotta beneath feathers and an elaborate headdress.

"What a lovely white peahen," I said and blew her a kiss since it was impossible to hug someone while dressed this way.

"You look pretty good yourself Lizzy. You might think of making this your new style."

"I don't know," I said with a laugh. "These feathers are expensive."

"Oh, you don't have to tell me. Mine are all real!"

"Seriously?"

Carlotta nodded.

"Did you, like, collect them?" Inka asked.

I worried that Carlotta might take offense. I worried that Inka wanted her to. I still wasn't sure of Inka's intentions.

"Some," Carlotta said, her cheeks glowing. "But I bought most of them."

"I hear you have a lot of brothers and sisters," Inka said. "Are any of them single?"

"Are any of them good-looking might be a better question for you," Carlotta replied.

Inka turned to look at me. "You're right," she said. "I

do like her.”

Carlotta smiled, glad to have been discussed.

“My brother Bart. He’s thirty and single and dressed as a bird, and that’s the best I can do. I’ll introduce you! But first, let’s get some drinks.”

Carlotta and Inka fluttered off towards the bar and the rest of our posse, myself included, trailed behind. Carlotta got us all a glass of the ‘special punch’ and we toasted her fabulous party!, her beautiful costume!, her new freedom to be herself! Each toast spurred conversation and more drinking. We had formed a wide circle, to accommodate our feathered spreads, and we had to yell across it in order to be heard. After a while, we got tired of yelling.

Jonis and Patty turned to each other to add their newest thoughts on the bank campaign. It had taken off full force and they were launching a whole second round of promotions, which meant that they could hardly go an hour without bringing it up. “No shop talk,” I reminded them but they only laughed and continued on. Inka and Carlotta had gotten into the specifics of her brother Bart. His favorite football team. His favorite beer. What kind of little brother he had been. I clicked together the soles of my white high heels. They were not very comfortable and neither was I. I liked to sit down, cross my legs and arms, and ball myself away at social events, and with a large peacock spread, sitting down at all was impossible.

I looked across the room to distract myself and caught the eye of a man looking right back at me. He waved, and this time, though he was dressed up in scattered brown feathers, and his dreadlocks were shorter and hung down over his shoulders instead of being pulled back, I knew him immediately. We were pulled together into the middle of the room and he reached out and shook my hand.

“I don’t think we were ever formally acquainted,” he said. “I’m Anthony Wendo.”

"The bird artist!" I nearly jumped on him.

"Yes, birds. I told you I was photographing birds."

"Yes. No. I didn't know you were THE bird artist. I saw your paintings at Korova."

He smiled like he knew how much those paintings of his had set in motion, though he couldn't possibly have.

"That Carlotta makes one beautiful bird," he said.

We both looked over at Carlotta, chatting with Inka, bobbing her head and shoulders as she laughed. Every bit of her awkward human form was alleviated; she looked just right.

"I better get back to my group," I said and turned to walk away. "Hey, did you ever find that shot?" I asked. "The bird reflecting in a window."

"Not yet. But don't you worry. I'll find it."

I went back and stood by Jonis and Patty, still chatting away about work. But before too long, Bart and his older brother Jim wandered over to the bar and as Carlotta pointed them out to Inka, the collective interest rekindled. We all turned to check out Bart. The possibility of two people coming together would always be interesting, no matter how many times it failed. I noticed his nose first. It pointed at the tip like Carlotta's. His costume was minimalist, a feathered eye mask and what looked like angel wings with a few blue feathers glued on. Broad shouldered and muscular, he should have looked funny in the small angel feathers, but he wore the costume easily. He threw his head back in laughter and then gave Jim a high five. Jim wore a teal sweat suit with feathered fans stuffed into the sleeves so that his arms ended not with hands, but with a spread of feathers. His face was painted intricately, likely Carlotta's doing, so that he looked like he belonged at an old carnival.

Our group crept close enough to hear what was being discussed at the bar between the two brothers. Close enough for Inka to intervene if she chose to.

"The idea of fame is full of contradiction. We love to

love stars, love to hate them. People work so hard and then they can't control themselves. Drug overdoses or being kicked out of the Olympics for being in a bar fight," Bart said, eyeing us, a crowd of strangers. He found his sister there among us and winked at her.

Carlotta leaned up against the bar and ordered a round of whiskey. "On me," she said.

"That's not a contradiction. It's all part of the stage. Broadway, the NFL, the Olympics, reality TV. It has nothing to do with honor, only getting noticed."

"The Olympics though? Isn't that more of an honor than a stage for fools? All that hard work?"

"And luck, and talent, and the desire to be recognized. All the same, you see. The more stages we offer, the more chances each of us will make it onto one."

The drinks came, the glasses passed around. Carlotta pushed a glass to each of her brothers, closing them into our circle.

"We're talking about the double life," Jim said. "The drive for fame. Like you, sis."

Patty's lips fuddled about her face, preparing words for Carlotta's defense. But Carlotta only smiled.

"Jim was always jealous of the attention I got as a child," Carlotta said with a laugh and pushed at her brother's shoulder.

"The only girl," he said. "Such luck!"

"The only peacock," Bart added with a laugh, the kind it was impossible to know the nature of – facetious, nervous, kind?

"I don't know about that," Inka said, sidling up to Bart. "I see several lovely peacocks here tonight." Inka swayed. Nerves or alcohol or the weight of her feathers? Bart took her arm to steady her. His hand lingered until he knew she was safe.

"I can get the local coverage," Jim said to Carlotta. "I do nightly news on TCN," he said to the rest of us.

"That's not at all the point, dear."

"We could write a play of it," Inka said. *"Pe-Foul Play."*

Bart laughed, again in his ambiguous way.

"That's not a bad idea," Bart said.

"I think Jonis has already started it," Inka replied.

"How'd you all get to know my sister again?" Bart asked.

"I saw a painting inspired by your sister and I was interested in writing about her, on the topic of living 'differently,'" Jonis said.

"Aha!" Jim said. "Fame."

"No, not like that. Not for publicity, for myself. There was an English author, Thomas de Quincy…"

"Opium," Carlotta said.

"Yeah, opium. He was at a desolate point, addicted and broke, but he turned it. He wrote out of his addiction with a book about the very thing he was addicted to. He used the thing holding him back to propel him forward. They say he suffered from something called trigeminal neuralgia, sharp facial pains so severe that they sometimes drove sufferers to suicide. We all have something to suffer from, to propel us. Maybe the opium helped him with the pain, maybe it made him everything he ever was."

"It killed him. The opium eventually killed him," Patty said, irritated by a speech both she and I had heard before.

"Shouldn't we all be so lucky as to die by our eccentricities?" Carlotta added.

The conversation had grown morbid and Inka tried to put a stop to it.

"PeeeeeeeeeeFoowwwwwwl," she said, turning the word to be like the sound the animal itself made, an *A*, sharp and squeaky. I smiled, a thank you, and Inka's body wavered, spilling some whiskey on Bart's feet.

I wasn't sure why she was suddenly acting so drunk. I was reminded of the time that she first met Jonis and the act she had put on, but she didn't seem to be acting tonight. Maybe I'd grown too far away from her to figure her out. Maybe this was her new technique of flirting.

"PeeeFoooowl! PeeeFooowl! The writer with the opium! The woman who's a peafowl! The man with the leg!"

"What is it then?" Bart asked of Jonis. "What's with your leg?"

"It's my thing," Jonis replied.

Inka nodded and gave Jonis's crutch a friendly tap with her glass.

Bart and his friend were momentarily mesmerized, staring at Jonis. It had been a while since I watched new faces, the nuances of the complete unknown. A tongue pushed on the inside of a cheek, an eyelash from the upper set creased over to the lower.

"What's it look like?" Bart asked.

"He doesn't like to discuss it," Patty said.

Jonis turned to Patty. "Don't. This is a gathering about being honest..."

Patty looked scolded.

"It's a disease I was born with. It's long, really, really long."

"Cool," Bart said.

Patty took a sip of her drink and scoffed. It was a mean noise, condescending and trite. I was suddenly sick of her. A turn. Jonis had this leg. It was real and it was hurting him. It wasn't romantic or idealistic, there to serve as a lesson for the rest of the world to learn politeness. I may not have always known this, I certainly didn't know it when I met Jonis, but I knew it now. Bart's question and response had been true. They came from interest, even sympathy. What was wrong with that?

"He's no freak show," Patty said. "So you can all stop staring."

Everyone but Inka quickly averted their eyes from Jonis. Inka kept right on staring at his leg as she leaned onto Bart's shoulder. He had a slim body and inviting eyes but it was impossible to tell if there was actually a person that Inka would consider "good-looking" underneath that costume. I took a step back from the wide circle. I had lost control of the conversation. I had no idea what would happen next. My shoes were digging into my feet and the feathers had begun to itch at my neck and the top of my head. I squirmed in my costume and tapped with my fingers at the spots causing the most irritation. What a burden birds had to bear, constantly being poked by the ticklish tuffs of feathers. I had never considered it. I could see now why my dad's birds were always picking at themselves with their beaks and feet, and why they habitually fluffed out their feathers, shook around, and then pulled them back in again, spreading feathers all over the place. It made me feel that I should dress up as every kind of animal in order to correctly understand their plights.

"He'll be dragging it around forever," Inka said wistfully. "And Lizzy will be dragging around the both of them."

And there she was – the Inka I'd been waiting for all night.

Patty's face was bright with anger. She looked at me as if to prove I had brought this all on. She looked young. Not like a mother but like a woman desperate and determined. I wished that my own mother could transform for me as easily as Patty did. I wished that I could see my mother as brave. I wanted to.

"He's going to have it amputated," I said to Inka and Patty both.

The circle paused, the air absorbed my words. It was hard to gauge facial expression with paint and masks. I thought that I should have something soothing to add, but I searched and nothing came. Patty was standing next to me. She looked at me. She grabbed my hand. Did she know I had caused this decision? I thought, at first, her grasp was meant to pull me down, but when it failed to, I decided that she needed me – to steady her, to help her understand. I held her hand tight and interlaced my fingers with hers.

"Damn," Bart said. "That's intense. Hell of a story! When does it come off?"

"A few months," Jonis said. He was looking at me and only me. I wanted to cry but I wouldn't let myself. "There's a bunch of consultations first. I've got to prepare."

"I can't even imagine it," Bart said. "They just hack it off?" He made a sawing motion.

Carlotta glared at him and he held up his hands as a sign of his innocence.

"It's a really brave thing…" Carlotta said to Jonis. I could tell she had more, but Inka suddenly buckled at the knees and landed on all fours on the ground, her feathery rump sticking right up into the air.

Bart and Carlotta picked her up and she smiled apologetically, glad the attention had turned to her.

"What's wrong with you, Inka?" I asked. Maybe the question should have been, 'Are you okay?' but I was already beyond that.

"You should keep your drugs out of our apartment," she said. She giggled and straightened out a feather she'd bent in her fall.

"Those were Jonis's…"

"Finders keepers," Inka said. "I have something else to confess," she paused quite intentionally for dramatic purposes. "I'm sleeping with Joe." Inka giggled, maniacally, looping around a *C* two octaves above the middle.

I released Patty's hand and took a step forward to stand face to face with Inka who Bart and Carlotta were still holding up.

"You're not the only who can get what they want," Inka said. She looked so happy, strung out on the mix of Vicodin, 'special punch,' and revenge. "You don't have anything to say to me?"

What was there to say? I watched her waver, left and

right. It made sense now, her going away for the weekends so secretly, her haughty glares. Sleeping with Joe was her declaration that she didn't need me anymore. I could imagine her and Joe together, their bodies pressed neatly, fitting caverns and bumps like a puzzle. There had always been chemistry between them.

"He wanted me back," I whispered in the hopes that no one but Inka would hear me. "But I never loved him." This wasn't true, but it felt right to say it now that I'd never consider loving him again.

"That's it," Inka said. "Don't you want to punch me? Don't you want to scream? You're too nice, Lizzy. Why, Lizzy? No one appreciates that."

I took a step towards her with aggression. Inka pulled back but for me, nothing happened. I wanted no revenge. I just wanted to be done with her.

"One day when we were out on the porch," I started. "I thought that you might have been a peacock in your last life. I could picture you running around with all those beautiful feathers, squawking out demands and attracting your mates," I told her.

Inka laughed though I hadn't expected her to. Maybe it was my fault. If I had told her this earlier, if I had told her that I had begun to despise her, she may have listened, she may have changed.

"I'm sorry about telling Joe," Inka uttered quietly. "I really am."

I would never forgive her for taking away my ability to be honest with Joe and to end things the right way. My ability to make a firm decision, to choose a man who would suffer over one who would reign.

"But there are some things that need to be said," Inka continued. "There are boundaries." She looked at Jonis. He hadn't moved. Neither had Patty. Jonis and Patty stood awkwardly frozen side by side, if they turned towards each other they would weep. If they turned away from each other they'd explode.

"I really loved you, Inka," I said softly.

Inka nodded and wiggled herself from Bart and Carlotta's grasp. As she waddled away, I hoped that she'd have enough sense to call for a cab instead of trying to walk all the way back through town and up the dark side streets dressed as a peacock.

"Forgive me?" I asked Carlotta. "I didn't mean to steal this wonderful night from you in any way." And then oddly, I felt that I should ask Bart as well. "Forgive me?" And Jonis and Patty. Most of all Patty. "Forgive me?" I asked Patty. "Please?" She looked at me longingly, like she wished she could kill me or be me.

I spun as I spoke. And once I'd asked them all, I continued still to spin. The air floated in-between my feathers. "Couldn't we all pretend to fly?" I asked Carlotta and she seemed to like the idea.

"If we can play your song," she said.

I reached inside my purse and handed her the CD I'd recorded for her and I felt a rush of nerves. She and I were the only ones who had heard it.

Carlotta made a lovely speech that like most speeches rambled on a bit too long. In the end, she invited everyone to "fly around the room as you listen to a song written for me by an understanding friend, the type of friend who makes living possible."

And every person there dressed-up and drunk as they were, skipped, hopped, chased, and fluttered around the room as my song played? I did my best to mimic the Dalcroze that Joe had taught me: my legs the beat, my arms the phrase, my head the breath. Jonis, on his crutches, moved about the steady beat. Patty splayed her arms like wings and slow with sorrow twisted them around. Carlotta with her freedom – would you believe that she lifted up off the ground and flew above us all?

CHAPTER TWENTY-TWO

We met in Petey's office, an uncluttered space. It had all the things an office should have and nothing more: a hardy dark-wood desk, neatly arranged curtains, a coffee pot half full on a table near the window. Petey shook Jonis's hand and then mine, a firm but friendly shake that left me feeling awkward – his eyes met mine, sadly?, and I looked away.

I had this strange fear-flash-fantasy of Petey pulling me aside at the end of the meeting, shutting his office door. "He's not going to make it," he says, and then catches me as I crumble, shriek, moan. "There's nothing I can do to save him," the imaginary Petey says. He presses his face up to mine, so close we could be kissing, we could be melting together. "I hope you can forgive me." I don't know why my mind ever wanders in such a sadistic way, or if this was some kind of uncontrollable premonition, but at the time it felt as far-fetched as an imaginary affair with a movie actor. It hardly fazed me at the time. Though in hindsight the memory sickens me deep in my stomach as if this imagining had opened a door for the darkest of fears to sneak through, a passageway to reality.

Petey offered us a seat in the chairs opposite his desk,

facing his hanging achievements: a neat row of certificat-
ions and doctoral awards and a blown up picture of Petey
and his attractive girlfriend posed before the Grand
Canyon at sunset. The other three walls were bare, white,
devoid of texture or design, a striking contrast to the walls
in Dr. Kershner's office where generations of children had
scribbled their admiration onto colored construction
paper. Several of Jonis's own creations hung on Dr. Kershner's walls – Jonis's favorite, centered above the patient
couch, was a porcupine hugging a bunny rabbit adorned
with band-aids, with the banner: "A great doctor can mend
anything." Petey didn't have such history supporting his
authority. He was no old-time virtuoso. He was a peer, a
person I may have acquainted at a friend's party. The kind
of man Inka would have approved of.

It's an odd adjustment when the people you must
trust your life with are suddenly the same age as you, when
for so many years there has been that comforting barrier in
having your doctors and nurses, car mechanics, teachers,
etc., separated by that distinction of time. The reassurance
of years making them smarter: *certainly they must be more sure,
must make fewer mistakes than I do*. And then suddenly it's
gone, you're no longer the child, and you have to go ahead
and trust someone who has been privy to only the same
number of years in the world as you or maybe a few more,
who likely doubts themselves, their choices, their understanding of life, as often as you do. What a difficult task.

Jonis pointed at the picture of the Grand Canyon.
"Such a deep hole," he said. "I've heard that people stand
before it and are compelled to jump in."

"I don't know," Petey stuttered.

"You weren't compelled?"

"It was beautiful."

"I'd like to see it someday. And I'd love to meet
Marta. We should all go out."

Petey smiled politely and opened up a folder that sat
centered on his desk.

"I'd like to go over the procedure," Petey said. His eyes kept shifting up and down nervously. Had he rehearsed this speech in the mirror at home before he came? Or, had he given it so many times before that it came out with no effort at all?

"Go ahead then," Jonis prompted.

"We'll be cutting below the knee…"

"Is that coffee hot?" Jonis asked.

"Yeah," Petey said. "I'll get you a…"

"I'll get it."

Jonis crutched across the room and poured a mug-full for himself and one for me as well.

"You can go on," Jonis said.

Petey looked at me and smiled, waiting for my permission or buying time so Jonis could return to his chair and listen properly, respectfully. I zipped my sweater all the way up to my neck line. "Cold today," I said, and Petey nodded.

"The bone in the tibia is cut 12-15 centimeters below the knee joint. This produces a good size stump to which a prosthesis can be fitted."

Jonis added cream to his cup and then to mine. Petey talked on about recent cases of amputation's succeeding in other KTS (Klippel-Trenaunay syndrome) and Weber syndrome patients with situations similar to his own.

"You're young and healthy," he said, "the greatest risk we're going to face is keeping away infection in the limb after surgery, which you are more susceptible to due to your blood-flow complications."

Jonis decided to add a little extra cream to my cup of coffee. I took it light. I watched him from my chair, the quick motions of his fingers, his casual lean upon his right crutch. I squirmed at Petey's words as they entered me: "clamp the major blood vessels," and Jonis added sugar to our coffees, took a sip of each to see that it tasted right.

Jonis carried the mugs over to us. Crutching and holding them, an ability he had mastered. His steps were so deliberate. He handed the cup to me and I took a sip, sweet and warm. It must have been strange for Jonis to have me by his side when it had always been Patty there with her domineering confidence. I was nothing like that. I sat nervously clenching my hands between my knees as Petey's descriptions went on and on.

"Have you told her yet?" Petey asked at the end of his monologue. "Your mother."

"Yeah. I told her."

Petey nodded. He thought for a moment, deciding on a story, then he looked at me. "It was my father who started the fire," he said to me. "The one that burned my entire back, my arms, and the back side of my legs. He came home late, drunk, left the burner going on the stove after making himself some scrambled eggs, and then went to sleep. My bedroom was next to the kitchen and by the time I woke up the fire was everywhere."

Now he turned his gaze and his story to Jonis.

"You're lucky, Jonis," he said, "that you don't have anyone to blame, not anyone human anyway, and I want you to keep it that way. This whole thing is up to you. You can change your mind at any time as long as you're changing it because *you* want to, not for anyone else."

"I'm going to do it, Petey," Jonis said. "I have to do it." He was not a man who changed his mind once it was made up.

We listened to the radio on the way home, not the college radio that we usually tuned in to for new aspiring musicians but the oldies station where we heard the songs our parents had imparted to us. We turned it up and sang loudly to Uriah Heep, and tried not to look at each other. There was something large between us now and it was difficult to adjust to the bloating. We'd made it from the city all the way back into to Tompkins County before I decided to speak.

I lowered the Beatles into the background.

"Have you heard of acrotomophilia?" I asked. I'd spend hours at the library the day before, preparing myself for what Petey would have to say to us, reading through dense medical journals on operations and outcomes. It was all so difficult to focus on, but I tried to make each word mean something, mean anything to me, and in the midst of all my effort I stumbled upon a section on personal experiences, and this errant word was the one thing I could remember.

"I've come across it."

"Extremity. To cut. To love," I said as if reciting.

"It doesn't sound so bad when you put it that way, instead of people who will only have sex with amputees."

"I plan to become a sufferer…if you want me to?"

Jonis laughed. A big sad hearty laugh that came from deep inside, from dark inside. A laugh from a future that would never come to be, or maybe from a past he would never know, maybe a laugh from a man whose genetics he shared, a man that he would never meet or even know the name of. The laugh concluded to silence. I could hear the differing pitches of our inhalations and exhalations. I swerved to avoid a garbage can rolling into the middle of the road. We were nearly home.

"Would you mind if we stopped for a few minutes?" I asked. "I want to take you somewhere, unless you're tired. It's totally fine if you're tired. I was going to do this another day, but now, well, now I'm feeling like doing it now, if you're up for it."

Jonis cleared his throat grown hoarse from that laugh. "Where to?" he asked.

"Here," I said.

We pulled off the road onto a gravelly side-strip and I shut off the car.

"Put on your gloves, it's cold out," I said and threw him the wadded ball of them. "And don't ask questions."

There was nothing around us but dirt covered hills

and barren mountains. The snow had melted and the ground was hard. Jonis's crutches made a crunch when he pressed them in. The trees on the mountains danced naked, arching bony limbs in the winter breeze. Against the blue sky and the sun's glare they looked like men, hundreds of desolate starved men, gathering together to keep warm. It might have been nice to join them, but I had other plans.

"This way," I guided him. "Here it is."

When I'd come out searching with my tape measure, I'd paid close attention to the hill's surroundings so I'd be sure to find it again. There was a small cluster of trees near the bottom, and when standing in front it lined up with the peak of a mountain in the distance. This hill was not much different than the other hills around us on the country road. It was patched in dirt and brown old grass. It rose slow and round and then fell back down again. But it had taken me hours to find this one hill. This perfect hill. Just when I thought that my idea had been dumb and I might as well give up, there it was.

"Walk to the top," I told him.

"Is this a joke?"

"I said no questions."

"A surprise party?"

"Just you, me, and a hill. Surprise!"

I instructed Jonis to stand in the center of the hill. I unfastened his sling and he smiled as he came to see my intention. I pulled his leg out of its bag and began to unroll it. I felt his softness between my hands and held tight to that skin that could not feel yet so entirely trusted me. I moved backwards down the hill and when I reached the bottom I placed his foot onto the ground.

Jonis threw down his crutches and hung his arms freely at his side. I stepped back to see all of him. He was his own sort of tree, sprung of the hard winter dirt and set against the grey sky. His brown sweatshirt, faded blue jeans, and pale skin sunk into the landscape and in the dull palate only his eyes were bright, blue and watery like fish scales.

"Hey," he called down to me.

"Hey."

"How did you do this?"

"I measured lots of hills."

"Come stand with me."

I climbed beside his leg until I reached the top. We held each other, crutch-less and tall.

"Before I left this morning, I caught my mother coming home from a yoga class. She told me that there was a woman with an artificial leg, said she did every pose. It was an advanced class, that's what she said. The woman painted the toe-nails on her prosthetic."

"Well, that's something," I replied. "In time, Patty will forgive us, right?"

Jonis nodded; he was so sure. "It's nice to be standing," he said. He kissed my forehead. "Thank you, Lizzy."

A hint of sun broke through the hazy clouds and tingled my skin. I released Jonis's waist so that he could stand, alone. He was a perfect man on two perfect legs. I will always remember him this way.

THE END

ABOUT THE AUTHOR

Catie Jarvis is an author of fiction, as well as a yoga instructor, a competitive gymnastics coach, and an online writing instructor at Southern New Hampshire University. She received her B.A. in writing from Ithaca College, and her M.F.A. in creative writing from the California College of the Arts. She grew up on a lake in northern New Jersey and now lives by the ocean in Santa Monica, California.

Her fiction can be found anthologized in *Writing that Risks* from Red Bridge Press, *Live Free or Undead* from Plaidswede Publishing, and in the online literary journal *Rivet.* Catie finds the world to be a strange place and loves writing that examines the ambiguity of "reality."

ABOUT HYPERBOREA

Hyperborea is an independent book publisher based in Canada.

Visit us online at hyperboreapub.com, and follow us on Facebook and Twitter (@HyperboreaBooks).

Read more. Read better.